Michelle's MEN

Lynn LaFleur

ELLORA'S CAVE
ROMANTICA PUBLISHING

An Ellora's Cave Romantica Publication

www.ellorascave.com

Michelle's Men

ISBN 9781419956560
ALL RIGHTS RESERVED.
Michelle's Men Copyright © 2007 Lynn LaFleur
Edited by Raelene Gorlinsky
Cover art by Syneca

This book printed in the U.S.A. by Jasmine-Jade Enterprises, LLC.

Electronic book Publication May 2007
Trade paperback Publication June 2007

Excerpt from *Destiny by Design* Copyright © Wylie Kinson, 2007

Content Advisory:

S – ENSUOUS
E – ROTIC
X – TREME

Ellora's Cave Publishing offers three levels of Romantica™ reading entertainment: S (S-ensuous), E (E-rotic), and X (X-treme).

The following material contains graphic sexual content meant for mature readers. This story has been rated E–rotic.

S-*ensuous* love scenes are explicit and leave nothing to the imagination.

E-*rotic* love scenes are explicit, leave nothing to the imagination, and are high in volume per the overall word count. E-rated titles might contain material that some readers find objectionable—in other words, almost anything goes, sexually. E-rated titles are the most graphic titles we carry in terms of both sexual language and descriptiveness in these works of literature.

X-*treme* titles differ from E-rated titles only in plot premise and storyline execution. Stories designated with the letter X tend to contain difficult or controversial subject matter not for the faint of heart.

Also by Lynn LaFleur

ଞଚ

A Cupid's Work is Never Done

Ellora's Cavemen: Legendary Tails I (*anthology*)

Enchanted Rogues (*anthology*)

Happy Birthday Baby

Holiday Heat (*anthology*)

One Night of Pleasure

Rent-A-Stud

Two Men and a Lady (*anthology*)

About the Author

ՏՇ

Lynn LaFleur was born and raised in a small town in Texas close to the Dallas/Fort Worth area. Writing has been in her blood since she was eight years old and wrote her first "story" for an English assignment.

Besides writing at every possible moment, Lynn loves reading, sewing, gardening, and learning new things on the computer. (She is determined to master Paint Shop Pro and Photoshop!) After living in various places on the West Coast for 21 years, she is back in Texas, 17 miles from her hometown.

Lynn would love to hear from her readers about her writing, her books, the look of her website...whatever! Comments, praise, and criticism all equally welcome.

Lynn welcomes comments from readers. You can find her website and email address on her author bio page at www.ellorascave.com.

Tell Us What You Think

We appreciate hearing reader opinions about our books. You can email us at Comments@EllorasCave.com.

MICHELLE'S MEN

സ

Trademarks Acknowledgement

ဆာ

The author acknowledges the trademarked status and trademark owners of the following wordmarks mentioned in this work of fiction:

Coke: Coca-Cola Bottling Company, Inc.

Dillard's: Dillard's International, Inc.

Chapter One

෨

Both of them sent her hormones into overdrive. Two best friends. One with short blond hair, one with shoulder-length dark brown. One with a husky build, one a runner's lean build. One with chocolate eyes, one with piercing green eyes.

Nathan Turner and Andre D'Amato.

Michelle Cooper told her overactive hormones to behave so she could finish the interview. She was temporarily in charge of hiring new escorts for Coopers' Companions, the business she and her brothers owned. Normally wrapped up in spreadsheets and flower bulbs, she'd taken over the job while her older brother, Brent, recuperated from a nasty bout of bronchitis. She would've passed the job along to her oldest brother, Zach, but he'd left five days ago on his honeymoon and wasn't due back for two more weeks.

Brent getting sick at the same time as they'd advertised for more escorts was rotten timing.

Gathering herself, Michelle sat up straighter in her chair. Despite wanting to drool, she had to present a professional image. "I'm going to tell you what Coopers' Companions expects, then I want y'all to answer some questions. Agreed?"

Both men nodded.

"Good." Michelle interlocked her fingers and rested her hands on the desk. "Coopers' Companions is an escort service. We hire men to escort women to dinners, business functions, parties…wherever they might need to go. Our employees are companions. They are not prostitutes. We do not hire men who are simply looking for easy sex. If that's why you're here, we have no reason to continue this conversation."

She looked from one man to the other. They both remained silent. Taking that as a sign that they were still interested in the job, she continued. "Whatever you do on your own time is your business. If a client decides she wants to spend more time with you after her business function, that's entirely up to you. Our escorts do not make the first move. It is totally up to the woman if she wants a more…intimate ending to the evening. Many of our clients are in their fifties and sixties, divorced or widowed, with high paying, executive positions. They only want an escort, nothing more."

Once again, she looked from one man to the other. She still held their attention. "Other women may ask you for sex. Again, that is up to you. As long as you are courteous, charming, and attentive to our clients, you need not take the evening any further than you wish. Our clients hire our escorts knowing all the rules. A woman will not be angry should you decline her offer for sex. If she *did* become angry, she would never be able to use our services again."

"But if we accept," Andre said, "that is not against your rules."

The sound of his accented voice sent a shiver down her spine and straight to her clit. Italian perhaps? Or maybe Greek. Combined with that gorgeous mane of dark hair and piercing green eyes, it made her want to lie down and spread her legs.

Damn David for breaking up with her last month. She hadn't wanted to move in with him. That wasn't a reason for him to break up with her, not in her book. She'd gotten used to regular sex. Finding another lover wouldn't be easy with her busy work schedule.

She again told her randy hormones to behave as she shook her head. "Your evenings are your own after you've fulfilled your obligation as an escort."

"Is there a rule about tips?" Nathan asked. "Are they offered, and if so, do we accept or decline?"

"Yes, the women often tip, Nathan, and they're very generous. Anything you make on top of your fee is yours."

Michelle pushed her hair behind her ears. "Those are the most important rules, and they're set in stone. Any questions?"

They shook their heads.

"*I* have a question. Why do y'all want to work for Coopers' Companions?"

"We have recently moved to Fort Worth from Chicago," Andre said. "We did not want to experience another snowy winter. Nathan and I have been friends for years and wish to work at something together. He saw your ad in the newspaper. It sounded like something we would enjoy." A teasing smile turned up his lips. "What man would not enjoy spending an evening with a lovely woman?"

Michelle melted. Everything inside her turned to liquid when Andre smiled.

If his smile affected her so strongly, she wondered how she'd feel if he kissed her.

"I agree with Andre," Nathan said. "We both enjoy the company of women. Being an escort seems like a natural job for us."

"You sound like my brother Zach. He believes every woman is beautiful in her own way."

"Your brother is an intelligent man," Nathan said, also smiling.

Ohmigod, his smile is as sexy as Andre's. Life simply isn't fair.

An image flashed through her head. All three of them naked and sweaty, writhing on her bed. Or on the floor. Either place would be fine. Nathan sucked her nipples and played with her clit while Andre licked her anus.

Mmm, nice fantasy.

But one that wouldn't come true. She didn't believe in mixing business with pleasure. It wasn't easy. There were some seriously hot guys working for Coopers' Companions. A healthy young woman couldn't help but be affected by all the testosterone in the air.

Besides, she'd never been involved in a *ménage a trois*. It sounded like fun when she read about one in a book, especially when it included double penetration. In real life, she wasn't sure how all the body parts...fit.

Michelle cleared her throat. "As for your salary, the client pays for the evening with her credit card when she calls in to hire one of our men. I write out paychecks on Monday. You'll receive a set fee for each woman you escort. I start all new escorts at our lowest fee, but that can rise quickly depending on how many clients you take out and their comments. Happy customers mean more money in your pocket. Courtesy has built our reputation. We won't accept an escort hurting or disappointing a client. Too many complaints and you're unemployed."

Nathan nodded. "We understand."

She looked from one man to the other. The women would be fighting each other to get hold of these two.

A trickle of jealousy crawled up her spine. How silly. Michelle had never become involved with one of the escorts and never would. As the only woman in the business and with twenty men working for her, she couldn't take the chance of any of them believing she was showing favoritism to one man.

Or two.

"So, any questions?" she asked.

"Just one," Nathan said. "When do we start?"

"I'm willing to set up a couple of dates and see how things work out. Is that acceptable?"

"That's fine with me." Nathan looked at his friend. "How about you, Andre?"

"A trial is acceptable to me also."

Michelle smiled. "Great. I try to give my escorts plenty of notice so they can plan their schedules, but last minute things pop up." She looked back at their applications. "You both have cell phones. Good." She placed their applications into a folder and stood. "I'll show you around the house. My brothers remodeled it. They tore out the wall between the kitchen and dining room and made a large meeting room."

Leading the way, Michelle walked down the short hall and into the meeting room. An oval oak table surrounded by twelve chairs sat in the middle of the room. "We rarely have all the escorts here at one time, but I have folding chairs if there are more than twelve." She gestured toward a large calendar on the wall. "If there's a particular day you need off, you write it here on the calendar. If you don't request a day off, I'll assume you're available and schedule you if you're needed. The weekends are naturally our busiest times. I ask my escorts to be available Friday and Saturday if at all possible."

No arguments. Michelle didn't think she'd ever interviewed two more agreeable men.

"This," she said, touching a wooden organizer hanging on the wall by the calendar, "is the message center. Each of my guys has his own cubbyhole. I'll put phone messages here, your paychecks, anything that is yours. If you're busy on Monday, your check will be here when you do come in. I've never had anyone take anything that didn't belong to him."

"You're lucky," Andre said.

"I have good guys working for me."

Standing this close to them, Michelle caught a whiff of woodsy cologne. She didn't know if Nathan wore it or Andre. Or perhaps both. The scent wasn't overpowering, but enticing.

Damn you, David.

"Well, if there aren't any other questions, we're done. As soon as I get proof of your physicals, I'll set each of you up with a client."

Andre took her hand and kissed the back. "It was a pleasure to meet you, Michelle. I look forward to a long and satisfying relationship with you."

Michelle had to concentrate to keep her eyes from crossing. Gorgeous, a sexy accent, and old-world manners. A woman couldn't ask for more.

She looked at Nathan. He winked at her. Well, okay, he'd work, too.

Clearing her throat, she gently pulled her hand away from Andre. "I'll call as soon as I arrange a date."

＊ ＊ ＊ ＊ ＊

"So what do you think?" Nathan asked once he and Andre were in his SUV.

"I think she's gorgeous."

"That's a given. I mean about the job. What do you think about fucking some woman as part of your job?"

"Michelle said not every evening ends with sex. I believe that's true. Besides, it's no different than meeting a woman at a bar and taking her home."

"I guess."

Andre shifted in his seat and faced Nathan. "We've already decided this is what we need to do. The pay is good. Working in the evenings will give us time during the day for your photography and my writing."

Nathan started the ignition and turned on the air conditioner. "It's a lot different here than in Chicago. The climate, the people, the way they talk."

Andre smiled. "Ah, yes. I love her accent."

"*You're* one to talk about an accent. You left Italy when you were fifteen. Poured it on a bit thick, didn't you?"

"I wanted to charm her."

"You did. She was drooling."

14

He shrugged. "American women are suckers for a foreign accent. And I'd say she was drooling over you too. I saw the way she kept looking at your chest."

Grinning, Nathan ran his hand over his chest and stomach. "She recognized prime when she saw it."

"Mmm, yes."

Nathan's grin faded. He watched his friend's gaze travel over his shoulders, his chest, and down his stomach to his groin.

Andre licked his bottom lip. "Prime indeed."

Nathan's cock responded to the heat in Andre's eyes. It only took one look, one touch, for Nathan to get hard. "Don't start something you aren't going to finish."

Andre's gaze snapped back to his face. "Who says I'm not going to finish?"

Suppressing a groan, Nathan put the gear shift into drive and pulled away from Coopers' Companions. "We can't do anything while I'm behind the wheel."

"I remember a few times when I've sucked you off while you were driving."

Nathan couldn't suppress the groan this time. He clearly recalled Andre's warm lips wrapped around his cock, his tongue tickling the slit. He'd loved it. The chance that they could've been seen at any time had only made it more exciting.

The few times Andre had sucked him off in a vehicle, they'd been on less populated roads. Driving down an interstate at seventy miles an hour was not the place for a blowjob.

"Hold that thought until later, okay? We have to meet the real estate agent in twenty minutes."

"Twenty minutes is plenty of time." Andre slid his hand between Nathan's thighs and caressed his balls. "I haven't had your cock down my throat in almost two weeks."

Between the move from Chicago, getting settled into an apartment and looking for a house to buy, sex had ended up at the bottom of the to-do list. Nathan's cock was reminding him of that fact, growing longer and harder with Andre's stroking. He lifted his hips so Andre's hand could slide farther between his thighs.

"Yeah, that's the way," Andre said, his voice husky. He lowered the zipper on Nathan's jeans. "You know you want my mouth on you."

Nathan never bothered with underwear, so it only took Andre a moment to pull his shaft through the zipper's opening. He tensed, waiting for the first swipe of his lover's tongue.

It came across the crown...warm, wet, with a promise of more. Nathan lifted his hips higher. Concentrating on driving had never been more difficult. He'd rather drive his cock all the way down Andre's throat.

"Take it," he rasped, holding the back of Andre's neck. "You wanted it. Take it all."

Nathan gripped the steering wheel to keep the SUV in the lane when Andre slid his lips all the way down Nathan's hard flesh. He knew this was insane. The last thing he wanted to do was cause an accident and possibly hurt someone. He had to stop Andre before...

His lover began sucking hard.

"Aw, *shit*!"

Nathan's need was too strong to stop Andre now. Taking the next exit off the freeway, he pulled into the parking lot of a large warehouse store. He threw the SUV into park, grabbed Andre's head and began fucking his mouth.

Four years together had taught Nathan exactly what Andre liked, and vice versa. Nathan closed his eyes and leaned his head back, absorbing the warmth of Andre's mouth. His lover knew how to drag out the pleasure, or to quickly bring him to a climax. Two weeks of abstinence meant Nathan's orgasm wouldn't take long, no matter what Andre did.

It built in his balls, whooshed up and down his spine, and exploded out the end of his cock.

Nathan had to wait for his heart to stop pounding in his temples before he could open his eyes. He watched Andre lick the last drop of cum from the slit before he sat back in his seat. A smug smile crossed his lips.

"Delicious as always."

Nathan barked out a laugh. "Shit, man, you're trying to kill both of us."

"I didn't hear you complaining."

Scraping one hand through his short hair, Nathan glanced down at Andre's crotch. The outline of his hard cock was all too apparent. "What about you?"

Andre pressed his hand against his fly. "You can take care of me later. For now, we have five minutes to get to the real estate office."

"Right." Nathan stuffed his softening cock back inside his jeans and zipped them. "Let's go find a house."

Chapter Two

✖

"Coopers' Companions, this is Michelle."

"Hey, Chelle."

Michelle smiled at the sound of Zach's voice. "Hey, big bro! How goes the honeymoon?"

"Incredible. Jade is… Ah, Chelle, she's everything I could ask for in a wife. She's charming, gracious, funny, sexy. Make that *very* sexy. God, I love her."

"I know you do. So why are you talking on the phone with me when you should be with her?"

"She's taking a nap. We were up pretty late last night, then walked around most of Jamaica this morning. Jade is having a blast buying silly souvenirs for everyone."

Michelle shifted the receiver to her other ear. "Where are you going after Jamaica?"

"Puerto Rico."

"Then?"

"The Lesser Antilles. St. Croix, St. John's, Martinique…and other islands I can't remember right now."

"Does she know?"

"Nope. I'm having fun surprising her."

She knew that her brother had planned a special honeymoon for Jade. They'd started out in Miami, but after that he'd refused to tell Jade where they were going. He'd told her to pack for three weeks in the sun and promised her a honeymoon she'd never forget. It sounded like he planned to live up to that promise.

"How's the weather?"

"Perfect. Sunny, light breeze, highs in the low eighties."

"You'd better be taking a lot of pictures."

"Jade takes pictures of *everything*. She bought two extra memory cards for her digital. She's almost filled up one already. I'm probably going to have to buy more cards."

"They'll be horribly expensive on a tropical island, if you can even buy them there."

"So I'll buy her some disposable cameras if she needs them."

"And never complain."

"Of course not. I'll buy her anything she wants. But enough about that. How are you doing? I talked to Brent before I called you. He sounds terrible."

"He actually sounds better today than he did yesterday. I finally convinced him to go to the doctor and get drugs."

"Good girl."

"Things are great here. Busy, but I like that. I've interviewed several possible escorts who weren't quite right. You wouldn't believe some of the strange men who answered our ad."

"Yeah, I *would* believe. I've interviewed strange men too."

"I did hire two new escorts yesterday. *Major* studs. Our clients will love them."

"Major studs, huh? Do I hear a bit of yearning in your voice?"

Sometimes she wished her brother didn't know her so well. "Of course not." She swallowed hard after that lie. "I'm saying that from an employer's point of view."

"Uh-huh. I don't remember you describing Rod as a major stud when we hired him."

"That's because Rod is like another brother. Heck, *all* our escorts treat me like a pesky little sister."

"Everyone adores you, Chelle. Almost as much as I do."

Warmth swelled inside her at his sweet words. She was so lucky to have a brother like Zach. She loved Brent, despite his fly-off-the-handle personality, but Zach was so special to her. "I love you too."

"Um, nice. Jade just kissed my neck. Since she's up from her nap, I'd better go. Maybe I can convince her to go back to bed for something besides a nap."

Michelle rolled her eyes. "Did you have to tell me that?"

Zach chuckled. "Call David. Won't he take care of you?"

His comment made Michelle realize she hadn't told Zach about her break-up with David. She hadn't wanted Zach to worry about her while he was wrapped up in wedding plans. "Nope. That's all over."

"What? You broke up with him?"

"Actually, he broke up with me. He asked me to move in with him. I said no."

"You two have been together for several months."

"I know, but I wasn't ready for anything that…serious."

"Are you okay?"

"Yeah. He's a great guy, but I don't love him. I don't think he was serious about me either. He just wanted a live-in housekeeper with fringe benefits."

Zach laughed, then moaned softly. "Uh, Chelle, I gotta go. Jade is… I gotta go."

Michelle smiled at the husky sound of her brother's voice. "Sure. Y'all have fun."

Her smile faded as she hung up the receiver. She was happy for her brother, truly happy. Jade was perfect for Zach, despite her ten-year age advantage. But she couldn't help feeling a bit sad too. Men had flitted in and out of her life since she was seventeen. Now, at twenty-six, the prospect of someone to love didn't look any more promising than it had nine years ago.

Well, you're just being silly, Michelle. Twenty-six is far from old.

Zach had been thirty before he found Jade. Michelle could wait. She enjoyed the company of a man. She enjoyed the pleasure they gave each other with their bodies. But she wouldn't settle for anything less than the man of her dreams. She wanted that one man who made her heart pound with a single look.

Without warning, the image of Andre and Nathan filled her mind.

They looked so different, but both were seriously hot. If she was ever going to break her rule about not getting involved with the escorts, they would be the reason.

And that would be incredibly stupid.

Work beckoned, even if she'd rather daydream about hunky guys with huge cocks. With a sigh, she turned back to her computer and pulled up her spreadsheet program.

She heard the bell's tinkle, signaling someone had come in the front door. She wasn't expecting anyone, but wouldn't be surprised if one of the escorts dropped by, or her stubborn brother. It would be just like Brent to ignore his doctor's advice and come into the office.

Instead of her brother, she looked up to see Andre.

It was a good thing she was sitting down or her legs might have buckled. David had been her lover for almost six months and she'd never reacted so strongly to him.

He smiled. "Good afternoon."

"Good afternoon." Michelle swallowed to erase the raspy sound of her voice. "What can I do for you?"

"Nathan and I picked up our lab results this morning. I decided to bring them to you."

"Wow, that was fast."

'We did not want to make you wait."

He handed her a manila envelope. Michelle waited until he sat in one of the chairs before her desk, then unfastened the clasp and withdrew the paperwork. She recognized the name of a large lab in the hospital district at the top of the forms. A quick glance over the results showed her Andre and Nathan were extremely healthy.

"Is everything satisfactory?" Andre asked.

"Yes. Your lab work is perfect."

"We take good care of ourselves."

Michelle let her gaze slide across his shoulders and chest. Yes, they certainly did take *excellent* care of themselves.

Professional, Michelle. Act professional. "Thank you for bringing these by. I'll set up you and Nathan with clients as soon as possible." She slipped the forms back into the envelope. "I hope you realize requesting lab work in no way means Coopers' Companions assumes you'll be intimate with a client. I told you and Nathan that sex is not a requirement of your job."

"You do not have to explain anything to me, Michelle. Nathan and I understand all the requirements of our job, but you do want healthy men escorting your clients. Any employer would want that."

God, that voice. Deep, cultured, sexy. She could sit here and listen to his accent the rest of the night. And into tomorrow morning.

The telephone rang. "Excuse me."

It was as if the gods had read her mind. Josephine Rowe, one of Coopers' Companions' regular clients, needed a last-minute escort for an important business function tonight. President of one of the large local banks, she often called at a moment's notice. Michelle always did her best to accommodate the woman, even though Mrs. Rowe usually called late on Friday when Michelle's guys were already booked.

This Friday was no different. All of her escorts were already booked tonight and tomorrow night...except for her two newest ones.

"Just a moment, Mrs. Rowe." She placed the call on hold and looked at Andre. "This is one of my regulars. She needs an escort tonight for a business function. Are you interested?"

"I will be happy to work tonight."

Michelle smiled. "Great. Just a sec and I'll give you all the info."

Two minutes later, she hung up and pushed a piece of paper across the desk toward Andre. "Mrs. Rowe's home address and the address where the event is being held. If you need help finding either, there's a large map of the area on the wall in the meeting room. I'll help you find both."

"I would appreciate that."

"Do you have a tuxedo?"

He smiled. "Yes."

She could imagine how handsome he would look in a tux. She could imagine how handsome he would look as she took that tux off him...

Professional, Michelle.

She pushed back her chair and stood. "Let's look at that map."

Andre followed Michelle to the meeting room. He admired the gentle sway of her hips in the tight jeans. She had the type of body he loved—full breasts, wide hips, rounded buttocks. When he held a woman like Michelle, he knew he was holding a *woman*.

He pretended to study the map of the local area on the wall while she went into the kitchen for drinks. Instead, he kept sneaking peeks at Michelle. He hadn't seen a wedding band on her finger, although that didn't mean she wasn't involved with someone. He hoped not. He wanted to get to know her better.

A *lot* better.

He and Nathan had lived together as best friends and lovers for the last four years. That didn't mean they didn't also enjoy the feel of a woman's body. The soft skin, the gentle curves, the silken glide of his hard cock into a wet pussy. Andre loved all of it.

He didn't like labels of gay or straight or bi. He enjoyed sex equally with a woman or man. To Andre, that didn't make him different or "perverted". He was simply a man who enjoyed sex, and enjoyed it often. Luckily, his lover could get hard again almost immediately after coming. Since Andre recuperated quickly also, he and Nathan rarely stopped with one lovemaking session.

Andre loved the times when they would lie in bed, sucking and fucking the day away.

Nathan had been the only man in Andre's life since they'd met. Andre liked it that way. He had no desire for another man and couldn't imagine himself involved with any man but Nathan. They shared a special friendship, a special love. Andre had no intention of doing anything to mess up their relationship.

Bringing a woman into that relationship would only make it deeper, more special.

They'd tried. Andre winced when he thought about some of the women they'd been involved with over the years. Some had been fascinated by two men having sex. Most had run away when they admitted they were a couple. None had been "the" woman whom he and Nathan wanted to be with for longer than a night.

Giving up the pretense of studying the map, Andre turned and watched Michelle place their glasses, spoons and container of sweeteners on a tray. She wore her long brown hair up today, with one of those ornate hair clips holding it in place. Tendrils drifted down her neck. He imagined following those tendrils up her neck to the sensitive spot behind her ear…first with his fingertip, then with his lips.

It had been a long time since he'd felt such a strong instant attraction for a woman. For that matter, he couldn't remember feeling such a strong attraction for *anyone* but Nathan. As soon as they'd met, Andre knew Nathan was his soul mate. There'd never been a doubt in his mind.

Perhaps he'd finally met the woman who would be a part of their lives.

"I hope iced tea is okay," Michelle said as she walked toward him with the tray. "I have soft drinks too, if you'd rather have that."

"Iced tea is fine." He took the tray from her and set it on the table. "I am not picky."

Andre waited until Michelle sat at the table before taking the chair beside her. He sipped his tea, enjoying the sharp bite of lemon. Too many people prepared tea weak and bland. Along with the lemon, Andre detected another flavor. "What type of tea is this?"

"Blackberry. Would you rather have plain? I can make some—"

"No, this is fine. It is very good." He sipped again, then set his glass on the table. "How did you and your brothers get into the male escort business? I doubt if it is the type of profession you dreamed of when you were a child."

Michelle chuckled. "That's true. Actually, my mother suggested it."

"Your *mother*?" Andre asked, surprised at her answer.

She nodded. "Have you heard of Wilcox-Doon Electronics?"

"Is that the company that makes calculators?"

"Calculators, radios, CD players…just about anything electronic. My mother is one of their vice presidents."

"An important position."

"Yes, one that requires traveling and dinner functions." She swirled her straw in her tea. The ice cubes tinkled against the glass. "My father passed away eleven years ago. My mother wasn't a VP at the time, but she was an executive who entertained quite often. We were talking in her bedroom one evening while she was getting ready to go to a stockholders meeting. I was only fifteen, but I remember that evening so clearly. My mom started crying and said how much she missed my dad, especially at times like this when she had to go to a business function without an escort."

She picked up a cookie from the tray and broke it in half. "I told my oldest brother Zach what she'd said. He was nineteen and in college, studying business management. He hated it. He had no desire for a degree or to be an executive. He liked the idea of a male escort service to help women like our mother who worked in important positions but had no man in their lives to accompany them to business functions. He told our mother that's what he wanted to do. She agreed to back him if he'd get his degree. That was important to her. So he worked hard, took extra courses, and graduated. He opened Coopers' Companions when he was twenty-one."

Andre sipped his tea, fascinated by the tale...and by the woman telling the tale.

"My other brother Brent was nineteen by then and wanted to be a partner. Zach made the same deal with him that my mother had made—degree first. That did *not* please Brent, but he did what Zach wanted. He took night courses to finish college while taking care of the business part."

"Nineteen is young for such an important position."

"Brent is a natural organizer. Zach is the charmer."

"And what are you?"

"I usually hide in my office and do the bookwork."

"So you like working with numbers?"

Michelle nodded. "Yes, but I'd rather be outside. I'm crazy about flowers and plants. I took over the accounting end of the business from Brent. He hated keeping up with the escorts' hours, paying bills, writing checks. I don't mind doing any of that."

Warmth spread through her cheeks when she realized she'd been monopolizing the conversation. "I'm sorry. You really didn't want the entire history of the company, did you?"

Andre smiled. "Actually, yes. I was curious how you and your brothers started what is obviously a very successful business. Plus, it gave me the chance to get to know you a bit better." Grasping the arms of her chair, he tugged it closer to him. "I'd like to get to know you a *lot* better."

How was any woman supposed to be able to think when she looked into those emerald eyes? She had to, though. She had to keep a level head and let Andre know her rules before he assumed their relationship could become more than business. "Andre, you're a gorgeous and sexy man. I'm sure you'll be a wonderful escort. But don't assume I'm part of the package."

"I would never assume anything, Michelle." His gaze traveled over her face, down to her breasts, back again. "I will admit I find you very attractive and would like to spend more time with you."

"As friends, fine. Nothing more."

He cocked his head to one side. "Why nothing more?"

"I don't get involved with my escorts. I made that rule a long time ago. I've never broken it."

A hint of a smile tilted up the corner of his mouth. "Ah, a challenge. I am a man who likes challenges."

"Don't even go there. It won't work."

"You do not know how determined I can be."

"That works both ways."

He leaned toward her, close enough so she could see her reflection in his pupils. Another few inches and his lips would touch hers. Michelle licked her lips in anticipation.

Instead of the kiss she expected, he tapped the end of her nose with his index finger. "I like you, Michelle Cooper. I believe you and I will be good…friends."

He pushed back his chair and stood. "I must get ready for my date. I will talk to you later."

Michelle watched him leave the room. A friend had never made her breathe funny. A friend had never made her heart gallop in her chest, or her tummy flutter. Only a lover had done that.

I'm in so *much trouble.*

Chapter Three

๛

The scent of coffee lured Andre to the kitchen. With his eyes half closed, he stumbled into the room and headed straight for the coffee pot. A chuckle behind him didn't make him pause for a second in his quest for caffeine.

"Good morning, Andre."

Two healthy sips. He only needed two healthy sips to get the blood to his brain so he could think. After that, he could enjoy his coffee while the rest of his body caught up with his brain.

He was definitely not a morning person.

Andre turned and leaned against the counter. Nathan sat at the small table, a newspaper open before him. He wore a pair of jeans cut-offs while Andre wore nothing. "You always say that. What the hell is so good about morning?"

"It's the start of a new glorious day."

"Shit."

Nathan laughed. "Is your bad mood because you're always grumpy in the morning, or a result of your date?"

"The date was fine." Andre topped off his mug and joined Nathan at the table. "Josephine Rowe is lovely, charming, has a great sense of humor. I'd guess her age to be around sixty." He took another sip of coffee. "The function was boring, as usual, but I enjoyed her company."

"You didn't wake me up when you got home."

Andre shrugged. "It was late and you were asleep. I was careful not to bother you when I got in bed."

"And?"

"And what?"

"Any…extracurricular activity?"

Andre shook his head. "She was content to feel me up through my trousers."

He grinned when Nathan almost choked on his coffee. "What?"

"She copped a feel every chance she had. I think she got off on the thrill of possibly being seen."

"Did she tip you?"

"She slipped a hundred-dollar bill into my waistband when I dropped her off at her house."

"Nice tip."

"Yeah." Andre set his mug on the table. "She said she would request me the next time she needs an escort."

"Sounds like you made quite an impression."

"It's the accent."

"And the long hair. A lot of women get off on a guy with long hair. Then there's the size of your dick, which I'm sure she noticed."

"I never got hard. Bigger, yes, but not hard."

"Hell, Andre, you're huge when you're soft."

"Are you complaining?"

"Hardly. I love every inch you have."

"The feeling is mutual."

That smoky look filled Nathan's eyes…the one Andre knew was a prelude to sex. While he'd love to take Nathan back to bed for a long suck and fuck session, he wanted to talk to him first. "What do you think of Michelle?"

The smoky look disappeared, to be replaced with confusion. "Michelle? You mean Michelle Cooper?"

Andre nodded.

"I think she's hot enough to burn up the sheets. Why?"

"I'm very attracted to her."

"That makes two of us."

"Really." Picking up his mug, Andre rose and walked to the coffee pot. He warmed his coffee, then carried the pot to the table to refill Nathan's mug. "So what do we do about it?"

"You thinking about asking her out?"

"Are you?"

Nathan glanced down at Andre's groin. "To be honest, it's difficult to think of Michelle right now when your dick is so close to my mouth."

Grinning, Andre shook his hips, causing his penis and balls to jiggle.

Nathan laughed. "Well, that completely spoiled the mood."

Andre bent over and lightly kissed Nathan's lips. "I'll be happy to get you back in the mood later." He replaced the coffee pot and returned to his chair. "We haven't been attracted to the same woman in a long time."

"Not since…what was her name?"

"Shelley."

"Yeah." Nathan rubbed his chin. His thumb rasped over the morning stubble. "I guess she didn't make much of an impression on me if I can't remember her name."

"It was over a year ago."

"We almost asked her to move in with us. I should remember her *name*."

Andre waved away Nathan's concern. "It doesn't matter. She wasn't right for us anyway. I think Michelle is."

"And you've figured this out from one meeting?"

"Actually, two. I spoke with her yesterday when I took her our lab results and she set me up with Josephine Rowe. She's charming and intelligent as well as beautiful."

"Don't forget built."

No, Andre wouldn't forget that. Those full breasts and rounded ass practically begged to be caressed. "There is one problem."

Nathan leaned back in his chair. "And that is?"

"She said she doesn't get involved with her escorts. Ever."

A devilish light twinkled in Nathan's eyes. "I do like a challenge."

"So do I, and I told Michelle that. She told me it wouldn't work, that she's very determined."

"Which is the same as throwing down the gauntlet."

Andre toasted Nathan with his mug. "Exactly."

"I assume you have a plan."

"We have to convince her to go out with us individually before we can admit we're a couple. I don't believe that will be a problem. I saw the way she looked at us Thursday during our interview. There was definitely interest in her eyes."

"Who takes her out first?"

"Whoever can convince her to go."

"Works for me." Nathan closed his newspaper and folded it in half. "I have an appointment with the agent to look at another house at eleven. Do you want to ride along?"

He could, but Andre trusted Nathan's judgment. Besides, he wanted some quiet time to work on his book. "You go. I'm going to write for a while."

"Okay. I'll grab a shower and get out of here."

Nathan pushed back his chair and rounded the table. When he reached Andre's side, Andre stuck out his hand and touched Nathan's hip.

"Any chance I could get you back in the mood now?"

The heat in Andre's eyes made Nathan's balls tighten. "There's a very good chance of that."

Andre slid his hand over Nathan's stomach and down the fly of his shorts. "Want company in the shower?"

Nathan arched his hips, wishing he could feel Andre's hand on his bare flesh instead of through the thick denim. He groaned softly when his lover squeezed his cock. "Always."

Taking Andre's hand, Nathan led the way to the bathroom. His shaft swelled with each step. He loved running his hands over Andre's soapy body in the shower. The water would often turn cold since they spent so much time pleasuring each other.

Nathan slipped off his shorts while Andre started the shower. He stared at Andre's tan back and buttocks. Andre loved to lie nude in the sun, so no swimsuit marks marred his body. The sight of that perfect body never failed to arouse him. Palming his cock, he slowly stroked it in anticipation of being buried deep inside Andre's ass.

Andre turned to face him. He looked at Nathan's face a moment, then his gaze wandered down Nathan's body. He smiled, slow and sexy.

"Looks like you're ready to…shower."

"Among other things."

Pushing back the shower curtain, Andre stepped into the tub. Nathan followed. He picked up the bottle of liquid soap while Andre moved beneath the spray. Nathan worked up a thick lather in his hands, then touched Andre's back. He spread the lather from Andre's shoulders to his buttocks. He took his time, enjoying the feel of his lover's flesh beneath his palms.

Andre tilted back his head and rested it on Nathan's shoulder. "Nice."

"Very." Nathan slid his hands around to Andre's chest and thumbed his nipples. "Love touching you."

"Me too." Andre moaned softly when Nathan rolled his nipples. "Yeah, that's good. Pinch them."

Four years together had taught Nathan when Andre wanted to make love and when he wanted to fuck. Perhaps part of Andre's excitement came from talking about Michelle, but Nathan recognized the signs. Right now, Andre wanted to fuck.

Picking up the bottle of soap again, he squirted the liquid directly onto Andre's skin. Slowly, he spread the creamy substance across Andre's smooth chest and down to his groin. He gripped Andre's hard cock and gently pumped it.

Andre released another moan and pressed his buttocks against Nathan's pelvis. "Fuck me."

Nathan kissed Andre's shoulder, the back of his neck. "Lean forward."

Andre braced his hands on the wall and spread his legs. With one hand still wrapped around Andre's shaft, Nathan coated his own cock and Andre's anus with thick lather. He lingered at the tight puckered hole, caressing it with one fingertip, then two. Andre hunched back at his fingers, as if asking for more. Nathan gave it, pushing one finger inside Andre's ass.

"Yeah." Andre groaned and arched his back. "Oh, yeah."

Never one to deny his lover's request, Nathan added a second finger. He pumped them in and out, in and out, as he caressed Andre's penis.

"Damn it, Nathan, *fuck me.*"

Nathan enjoyed the tenderness, the loving, he and Andre shared. Right now, tenderness wasn't on his list of importance. Apparently, it wasn't on Andre's list either.

He pressed the head of his shaft against Andre's anus. Andre blew out a breath and arched his back even more. Nathan pressed forward slowly, so slowly, until every inch of his rod filled Andre's ass.

"God," Andre groaned.

"Mmm, yeah." Nathan wrapped his arm around Andre's waist and began to pump. His thrusts picked up speed as he continued to fondle his lover's hard flesh. "Love fucking you."

Andre grabbed Nathan's hand. "I'm close."

Nathan thrust faster, wanting to reach a climax at the same time as Andre. He felt Andre's body tremble, his anus contract, his penis jerk. Ramming his shaft as far inside Andre as he could, Nathan shut his eyes and let the pleasure overtake him.

Moments passed, the running shower and their heavy breathing the only thing Nathan heard. The warm water fell on his neck as he hugged Andre close to him. "Love you," he whispered.

Andre squeezed the hand still wrapped around his softening cock. "Love you too."

Nathan pulled out of Andre's body. "Turn around."

Andre faced him. Cradling his lover's face in his hands, Nathan kissed Andre. He tilted his head one way, then the other, as he kissed Andre again and again. Lips met, tongues touched, breaths mingled.

Nathan kissed the spot on Andre's neck that he knew was so sensitive before stepping back. "We'd better finish our shower before the water turns cold."

Amusement flashed through Andre's eyes. "No, cold water is not our friend."

Nathan dropped one more kiss on Andre's lips. "Turn around again and I'll wash your back."

The simple act of washing Andre's back gave Nathan almost as much pleasure as making love with him. Andre wasn't Nathan's first male lover, but Andre would be his last. Nathan had no desire to look at another man, much less take him as a lover. From the first time he had held Andre in his arms, he'd known there would never be another man for him.

A woman was another matter.

He and Andre loved women. They both wanted a woman in their lives. Their search for one hadn't been successful, but he didn't want to give up and he knew Andre didn't either. Perhaps Andre was right and Michelle would be the one they'd been searching for all this time.

"So you think Michelle might be interested in us?"

"Yes, I do."

"Do you have a plan?"

"Be charming, courteous, attentive." Andre flashed Nathan a grin over his shoulder. "Dazzle her with my accent."

"It's funny how that accent comes and goes depending on who's around."

Andre's grin widened. "I'll see her Monday when I pick up my paycheck for last night. I'll talk to her then."

"Maybe I should tag along. Two can be more convincing than one."

"Sounds like a plan."

Chapter Four

ﮔ

Michelle had known some very nice men who were far from handsome. Good looks were pleasing, but they'd never been a factor in her deciding whether or not she'd date a man. A sense of humor meant more to her than a handsome face. Although all Coopers' Companions' escorts qualified for the hunk scale, they didn't make her hormones stand up and take notice. She'd known most of them for years and had become friends with them. Teasing remarks about her freckles didn't lead to drooling, despite their good looks.

Her brothers hadn't told her she couldn't date any of her escorts. She'd made that rule herself to avoid uncomfortable situations. It was important to her that all her guys felt equal with each other. If a client requested a particular escort, she would send him on the date. Otherwise, she kept a detailed chart and rotated the guys on dates so everyone had close to the same amount.

Everything had flowed smoothly until Andre and Nathan showed up.

She'd spent the weekend fantasizing about them. Slow kisses, gentle caresses, long licks, tiny nips. She'd imagined each of them doing all those things to her…and more.

And at the same time.

Michelle continued to stuff the guys' cubbyholes with envelopes holding their paychecks. She needed a distraction, something to do to get her mind off hormones and hunky men. Breanna immediately came to mind. Michelle had become fast friends with Jade's daughter as soon as they met. Although Breanna was four years her junior, Michelle had discovered she and her friend had a lot in common. As soon as she finished sorting the paychecks, she'd call Breanna and ask her to dinner tonight.

The sound of the front door opening and closing drew Michelle's attention. She glanced at the clock on the wall. Rarely did any of the escorts arrive this early for their checks.

"Michelle?" Brent called out.

She smiled when she heard her brother's voice. He sounded so much better than he had Thursday. "In here."

He stepped through the doorway, pushing his long blond hair back from his forehead. "Hey, sis."

"Hey, bro. You sound a lot better."

"I *feel* a lot better. I hate being sick."

Michelle knew that. Both of her brothers hated weakness of any kind. They'd coddle her or their mother, but didn't want to be coddled in return. "You haven't been sick in a long time. You were due."

"It's your fault."

"*My* fault?"

"Yeah. I caught your stupid cold and it settled in my lungs."

She would've bopped him if she hadn't seen the amusement shining in his eyes. He loved to pick on her. So did Zach. "It isn't my fault you didn't take care of yourself."

"I have to blame someone. You're convenient."

"Lucky for me."

Brent chuckled and tweaked her nose. "Any coffee?"

"You know there is. Are you making breakfast to go with that coffee?"

"You expect me to *cook* when I've been sick?"

"Yes, I do."

"God, you're mean."

Michelle grinned as she watched Brent walk into the kitchen. He always grumbled, but he loved to cook. Both her brothers were excellent cooks. Somehow, Michelle hadn't inherited that talent. Besides, cooking for one was no fun.

"What do you want to eat?" Brent asked.

"I'm not picky." She placed the last envelope in the appropriate cubbyhole, then walked over to the bar and slid onto a stool. "I'll be happy with scrambled eggs and toast."

"You got it." He opened the refrigerator and took out a carton of eggs. "So, what's been happening here while I was gone?"

"Same ol' stuff. Busy. I had everyone scheduled this weekend, except for Nathan."

Brent paused in the act of cracking an egg and looked at Michelle. "Nathan?"

"One of our new escorts. I hired two Friday — Nathan Turner and Andre D'Amato."

"You hired them without checking with me?"

Michelle frowned. "Since when do I need your permission?"

"Did you have them get lab work?"

"Yes."

"Did you run the background check?"

"Yes. And before you ask anything else, I did everything I'm supposed to do. I'm not a little girl, Brent. I'm an equal partner, in case you've forgotten that."

"I know that." He cracked the egg into a glass bowl and took another one from the carton. "You've interviewed lots of guys, but you've never hired any without checking with me or Zach first."

"Zach is on his honeymoon and you were sick. We need escorts. I told you I had everyone scheduled this weekend. With the holiday season coming up, we'll be busy every weekend."

Brent took a wire whisk from the utensil drawer and began to beat the eggs. "So tell me about these guys."

"They're both thirty-one and moved here from Chicago. Handsome, charming, articulate. Andre has dark hair, green eyes, olive skin. He has a runner's build, like you. Nathan is blond with brown eyes. He's built like Zach." She propped one elbow on the bar and rested her cheek against it. "Andre has the nummiest Italian accent."

Brent chuckled. "Nummiest?"

To Michelle's dismay, warmth flooded her cheeks. Talk about opening mouth and inserting foot. "He'll completely charm the ladies. So will Nathan. I think they'll both be very successful."

Taking a bottle of oil from the cabinet, Brent drizzled a small amount into the skillet. "Which one impressed you the most?"

"They'll both be great, Brent. I promise."

Brent moved the skillet from the burner, then bent over and rested his forearms on the counter. "Are you attracted to them?"

The warmth turned hotter. Michelle prayed her cheeks weren't as red as they felt. "I don't date the escorts."

"You aren't answering my question. Your voice is…different when you talk about these new guys."

Michelle started to push her hair behind her ears, but stopped herself. That telltale action would give away her nervousness.

"I've never said you couldn't date the escorts. Neither has Zach, to my knowledge."

"No, he hasn't."

"If you want to go out with one of these new guys, go for it. You and David recently broke up. Let Andre or Nathanial take you out and show you a good time."

"It's Nathan."

"Whatever. There's nothing wrong with you dating one of the escorts."

"Brent, the guys treat me like their little sister."

"That's because you treat them like your brothers. If you showed the slightest bit of interest, Peter would ask you out in a second. So would Daryl."

Peter and Daryl? They were hunks, but Michelle had never been physically attracted to either of them. "I don't think it's right to date the escorts. If I dated one, I'd have to date all of them to avoid any hard feelings or someone thinking I'm playing favorites."

"I don't believe you should date all of them, but one or two would be okay if that's what you wanted. It might be a good idea to see how they act on a date."

"We have a good group of guys. We don't get any complaints about any of them."

"It still wouldn't hurt to check them out."

Michelle folded her arms and propped them on the bar. "Does this 'checking out' you're talking about include sex?"

Brent quickly straightened. "I didn't say anything about sex. I said you should *date* them. There's a difference."

Michelle laughed. She should've known her brother wouldn't be so modern. "Brent, a date often means sex. This is the twenty-first century, you know."

He turned back to the stove. "I don't need to hear that."

"I'm not saying every date ends with sex. But if I'm attracted to the guy and he's attracted to me, then—"

"Michelle, I don't want to hear about your sex life, okay? You're my baby sister. As far as I'm concerned, you're still a virgin."

"Hardly. I haven't been a virgin for years."

"Shit," Brent muttered. He set the skillet back on the burner and picked up the bowl of beaten eggs. "Why do you tell me stuff like that?"

"Because it makes you crazy."

"You're cruel, Michelle."

Now that the subject of sex had come up, she didn't want to drop it. Brent had to realize she wasn't ten anymore. "How many women have you had sex with?"

"That's different and you know it."

"Why? Because a guy is a stud if he enjoys sex, but a woman is a slut?"

"I didn't say that!" Brent set the empty bowl on the counter with a loud *thump*. "How did this conversation get started?"

"*You* did it."

Brent removed a spatula from the utensil drawer and began to stir the eggs. "If I started it, then I can stop it. Did you get the paychecks done?"

"Yes, I got the paychecks done. Yours is in the desk."

"What about…"

He stopped when the front door opened and closed. Michelle turned on her stool. It had to be one of the guys coming for his check.

She almost swallowed her tongue when Andre and Nathan stepped into the room. Simple T-shirts and jeans had never looked so good. "Hi."

"Good morning," Nathan said, smiling. "Andre came to pick up his check and I decided to tag along."

He could tag along anytime he wanted to. Michelle drank in the sight of the two men as they walked toward her. Her heart picked up its beat, her breathing became heavier. She'd never been attracted to any of the other escorts, but her feelings were so different for Andre and Nathan.

"How about some introductions, Michelle?" Brent asked.

Warmth shot back into her cheeks at her brother's question. "Yes, of course. I'm sorry. Brent, this is Andre and Nathan. Guys, my brother Brent."

Brent rounded the bar and shook each man's hand. "Welcome to Coopers' Companions."

"Thank you," Andre said. "Nathan and I are honored to be part of your company."

"I'm making breakfast for Michelle and me. Join us?"

"I have an appointment in twenty minutes," Nathan said. "I'll take a rain check."

"Sure. Andre, how about you?"

"I am riding with Nathan, so I cannot stay either. But thank you." His gaze swung to Michelle. "May I have a word with you in private?"

Something must have gone wrong with Andre's date. She couldn't imagine any other reason for his wishing to speak to her privately. "Sure. Let's go to my office."

Michelle led the way with Andre by her side. The main office in the front of the house was where she and her brothers conducted business. When she wanted to work without interruptions, she chose her private office at the back of the house. Zach had converted what was once the master bedroom into an office for her so it still maintained the comfort of a bedroom—complete with daybed for lazy days with a good book—while including everything an office needed. It connected to its own bath, making it easy for her to work late and still get ready for a date or dinner with friends.

Once in the privacy of her office, she faced Andre. "Did something happen with Mrs. Rowe?"

"No. Josephine was a gracious lady. I enjoyed her company."

"Then what's wrong?"

"There is nothing wrong." He stepped closer and took one of her hands in his. Raising it to his mouth, he kissed the back of her fingers. "I wish to invite you to have dinner with me tonight."

The invitation completely floored her. Michelle hadn't expected Andre to ask her out since she'd told him she didn't date her escorts. He shouldn't even…

She drew in a sharp breath when he blew on her fingers. The man didn't play fair at all.

"Andre, I told you I don't date the escorts."

"I am new. Do not think of me as an escort yet."

"You've taken out one of my clients. You're officially an escort."

The tip of his tongue dipped between two of her fingers. Michelle had to concentrate to keep her eyes from rolling back in her head from pleasure.

"I will take you to the finest restaurant in the area. Your choice. We will dine, dance, get to know each other better. Then…" He sucked one finger into his mouth and ran his tongue around it. "We will see what happens next."

Michelle knew exactly what would happen next — she'd jump his bones. Before she gave in and did exactly that, she tugged her hand away from his. "I can't."

Andre gave her a crooked grin. "You cannot blame me for trying."

"I appreciate the offer, I really do. I just… The guys are my employees. I don't feel right dating any of my escorts."

"I understand." He took her hand again and kissed her fingers once more. "I am a determined man. I like you and I will not give up."

"I'll still say no."

"And I shall keep asking."

"I'd rather you didn't."

He leaned closer to her, his lips parted. Michelle caught a whiff of mint-flavored breath. She backed away before he could kiss her.

That crooked grin flashed across his lips again. "I think you are worth waiting for, Michelle, no matter how long it might take."

He left her standing in the middle of her office. Michelle placed one hand over her churning stomach, then slowly ran it down the fly of her jeans and between her legs. She moaned when she touched her clit. If she slid her hand inside her panties right now, she knew she'd find her clit hard and her labia swollen and wet. All it had taken was a few moments with Andre to make her hormones stand up at attention.

Needing a distraction now more than ever, she turned to her desk and picked up the receiver to call Breanna.

* * * * *

"I don't see the problem," Breanna said after taking a sip of her daiquiri. "You're surrounded by gorgeous men. Why *not* date them?"

Michelle scooped up salt from the rim of her margarita glass and licked it from her finger. "Wouldn't it be unethical? If I dated one, wouldn't that show favoritism?"

"So date all of them."

Michelle frowned while Breanna grinned. "Will you be serious?"

"Okay, okay. I don't see a problem. You know the guys. You like them and they like you. Go for it."

"You sound like Brent. He told me today I should date a couple of the escorts and see how they act on dates."

"You mean Brent actually said something *intelligent*?"

Michelle sighed. She didn't understand why Breanna and Brent were so hostile toward each other. "Why don't you like him?"

"I don't dislike him. Brent is…" She paused long enough to take a sip of her drink. "There's no better way to say this. Brent is a total chauvinist. That's hard for me to take."

"I think he's changed. He can still be a jerk, but he's crazy about Jade. He wants her and Zach to be happy."

"So do I. I'm glad Mom found Zach." Breanna smiled. "He can make her blush so easily. They're really cute together. She acts twenty years younger when she's with him."

"Have you talked to them since they left for their honeymoon?"

"A couple of times. Mom is having a blast. She loves surprises and Zach is…"

Her voice trailed off when her gaze strayed toward the front of the restaurant. Her eyes widened. "Whoa! Major hunk alert."

Michelle turned her head and glanced over her shoulder. Of all the restaurants in the Metroplex, they had to show up here. Fate wasn't kind at all. "I don't believe it," she muttered.

"What?"

She quickly faced Breanna again so the guys wouldn't see her. "That's Andre and Nathan."

"Your new escorts? The ones you have the hots for?"

"Sheesh, Bre, why don't you say that a little louder so the people in the back can hear you?"

"My God, Michelle, they're *gorgeous*. How can you keep from jumping them every time you see them?"

"It hasn't been easy, believe me."

Breanna licked her lips. "I'd take either one."

Propping her elbow on the table, Michelle laid her hand against her cheek to hide her face. "Please tell me they aren't coming this way."

"Can't. The hostess is leading them right toward us."

"*Damn* it!"

"You're hiding your face. They won't see you and they don't know me."

"Don't make eye contact, okay?"

Michelle should've known better than to ask the impossible of Breanna. She loved men and took every opportunity to flirt. She smiled up at Andre as he reached their table. He returned her smile before his gaze flashed to

Michelle. He stopped in his tracks and Nathan ran into his back.

"Look who is here," Andre said.

Nathan looked first at Breanna, then Michelle. A smile spread across his mouth. "Hey, Michelle."

"Would you gentlemen like to sit with your friends?" the hostess asked.

"Yes," Breanna said, "please join us."

Torture was too good for Breanna. Michelle narrowed her eyes at her friend. Breanna simply smiled sweetly and moved her purse from the chair next to her so Andre could sit down.

Nathan took the chair next to Michelle. "Having dinner with two beautiful ladies will be more fun than eating with Andre."

Michelle was still plotting ways to hurt Breanna, so didn't respond to Nathan's comment. She gasped when Breanna kicked her shin.

"Introductions, Michelle?"

Rubbing her shin with the back of her other leg, Michelle shot daggers at Breanna before summoning a smile for her escorts. "Nathan Turner, Andre D'Amato, Breanna Talmage. Bre is my brother Zach's wife's daughter." She bit her bottom lip when she realized how confusing that must have sounded. "Did I say that right?"

Andre laughed. "You said it fine. Breanna is your niece by marriage."

"I am?" Breanna frowned for a moment, then giggled. "I never thought of that! Can I call you Auntie Chelle?"

"Only if you want a black eye."

Both men laughed, and Michelle relaxed. This wasn't a date, so she had no reason to feel uncomfortable with Andre and Nathan. A simple dinner didn't mean she was breaking her rule about not getting involved with the escorts.

She was beginning to hate that rule.

The waitress came to the table to take their orders. Since Michelle hadn't opened her menu yet, she did this now while the men placed their drink orders. She felt a nudge on her abused shin and looked at her friend. Breanna rolled her eyes and mouthed the word "hot".

"Any recommendations?" Nathan asked.

"What are you hungry for?"

He looked into Michelle's eyes, the hint of a devilish grin on his lips. His gaze dropped to her mouth and lingered there a moment before he looked into her eyes again. "I'm open to anything."

"We're talking about food, right?"

"Are we?"

He licked his bottom lip. Michelle would swear his tongue flicked across her clit.

"I'm having the shrimp and pasta," Breanna said. "Michelle, order for me, okay? I'll be right back."

Both men stood when Breanna did. She flashed each of them a smile. "Such manners. I'm not used to that."

"You are not associating with the right kind of man," Andre said.

"That's for sure."

"If you are going to the ladies' room, perhaps you could show me the way to the men's room."

"Of course. Follow me."

Once Breanna and Andre left, Michelle turned her attention back to her menu to keep from looking directly at Nathan. She could see him watching her from the corner of her eye. Several seconds passed and he continued to watch her. Giving up all pretense of studying her menu, Michelle closed it and faced Nathan.

"You're staring at me."

"I like staring at a beautiful woman."

"Now I know you're pulling my leg. I'm not beautiful."

He wrapped one curl of her hair around his forefinger. "I have perfect vision. I know a beautiful woman when I see one."

He touched nothing but that one tendril of hair, yet Michelle felt his touch throughout her body. She wanted more. She wanted his lips on hers, his hands on her breasts, her pussy. She wanted his cock buried deep inside her…

Nathan leaned closer to her. "Do you know how expressive your eyes are? They're burning right now." He slid his hand beneath her hair. One thumb glided up and down her neck. "I want you, Michelle."

His bluntness made her even hotter. "I can't," she whispered.

"You can. We'll be so good together." Leaning even closer, he nipped her earlobe. "I want to touch you, feel your bare skin against me. I want to run my tongue all over your sweet pussy, then slide my cock into it. Take me home with you."

Her eyes drifted closed when the tip of Nathan's tongue darted into her ear. Right now, with her body so hot, she couldn't remember any reason she shouldn't take him home with her.

"May I join you?" Andre asked.

Andre's voice was like a glass of cold water thrown in her face. Cheeks flaming, Michelle pulled away from Nathan. "Of course. We were just…talking."

"Talking." Andre returned to his chair. "I would like to 'talk' to you that way, Michelle."

Michelle looked from one man to the other. She wanted both of them. She'd never been attracted to two men at the same time. If she had to choose between them right now, she wouldn't know what to do.

Breanna returned to the table. She gestured for the guys to remain seated before they had the chance to stand. "Did you order?" she asked Michelle.

"No." Her voice sounded as if she'd had a cold for a week. Michelle cleared her throat. "Andre and Nathan haven't had the chance to decide what they want."

"I will have what Breanna chose," Andre said, his hooded gaze still on Michelle.

"Sounds good." Nathan closed his menu without looking at it.

Her appetite had disappeared, but Michelle went along with the majority. Andre acted as spokesman when the waitress returned with his and Nathan's drinks, ordering dinner as well as a bottle of Chardonnay.

Always at ease talking, Breanna took over the conversation with Andre and Nathan. Michelle let her. Conversation had never been a problem for her, but she found herself unable to think with the two men so close to her. Nathan had scooted his chair closer to her so their thighs touched. Her own chair was up against the wall, so she had nowhere to go.

It amazed her how warm his thigh felt with two layers of clothing between their skin.

Andre stared at her. He'd look at Breanna to answer a direct question, but his gaze always returned to Michelle.

She felt surrounded by testosterone.

You're being really stupid, Michelle. It doesn't bother you to be around any of your escorts. It shouldn't bother you to have dinner with Andre and Nathan, especially since Breanna is here.

The pep talk and a glass of wine helped her to relax. By the time dinner was served, she was laughing along with the other three at the table. She ate every bite of her pasta and accepted Nathan's offer to share a piece of chocolate fudge cake for dessert. Breanna shared her cake with Andre, but declined the guys' offer to take in a movie.

"Sorry, but I have school tomorrow and have to study."

"Of course," Andre said. "Perhaps another time."

Breanna smiled. "I'd like that."

Michelle reached for her purse to pay for her meal. Nathan's gentle touch on her hand stopped her.

"Andre and I will take care of the bill."

"Oh. Well, thank you. That's very nice."

He winked at her. "It's our pleasure."

"Would you ladies prefer that we see you home?" Andre asked.

"That's so sweet and…old world," Breanna said. "I've been getting home on my own for a long time. But thank you." She looked at Michelle. "You ready to go?"

"Yeah."

Nathan quickly stood and pulled back Michelle's chair. Smiling her thanks, she picked up her purse and rose.

"Thanks again, guys. Bye."

"We will see you soon, Michelle," Andre said.

She led the way through the restaurant and out the entrance. Once outside, Breanna grabbed her arm.

"Ohmigod, they're yummy! And absolutely crazy about you."

Michelle released a snort of laughter. "Yeah, right."

"They couldn't take their eyes off you." She hooked her arm through Michelle's. "I should be angry. I'm not used to being ignored."

"They were both friendly and polite to you."

"*Pffft*. Friendly and polite don't equal interest. I thought one of them would ask me out. Nothing. Zip." She sighed dramatically. "It looks like the only date I'll have in the near future is with my vibrator."

"Thanks for that mental picture, Bre." Michelle dug in her purse for her car keys. "You've asked guys out lots of times."

"Only when they seem interested in me. Those two want *you*, Michelle."

Giving up the search for her keys, Michelle leaned back against her car. "The feeling is mutual."

"So why didn't you accept their invitation to the movies?"

"Because I didn't want to go without you. I can't go out with *both* of them."

"Why not?" Breanna leaned against the car next to Michelle. "Having two men at once is *amazing*."

Becoming good friends with Breanna over the last few months had meant sharing secrets, dreams, desires. This little tidbit of information was totally new to Michelle. "You've been with two men at the same time?"

Breanna nodded. "Once. Ohmigod, it was so hot. Four hands, two tongues, two cocks." She shivered. "Absolutely dee-lish."

"What did you do?"

"Everything."

"As in…everything? Including double penetration?"

"Oh, yeah. I *really* liked that."

Michelle placed one hand over her jumping stomach. "You're hurting me."

"Hell, I'm hurting myself thinking about it." She grabbed Michelle's hand. "Do *not* tell my mother."

"As if I'd tell Jade anything you tell me. Besides, you said you and Jade talk about sex all the time."

"We do. She's my best friend. But as free thinking as she is, I don't think she'd like the idea of her daughter being involved in a *ménage à trois*." Breanna shifted to face Michelle. "If you want those two guys, go for it. Forget your rule about not dating the escorts—which I think is a stupid rule anyway—and jump them."

Michelle pushed her hair behind her ears. "I'll think about it."

"Don't think, just *do*."

Breanna straightened from the car and gave Michelle a hug. "I gotta go study. Let me know what you decide to do."

Michelle watched her friend walk to her car before digging in her purse for the car keys again. She finally located them hidden beneath a package of tissues. Climbing into her car, she started the motor and flipped on the air conditioner.

Michelle leaned closer to one of the vents, letting the cool air flow over her moist, heated skin. It didn't help. She still felt hot, antsy.

Damn hormones.

Andre and Nathan filled her mind once again. She thought of what Breanna had said about her *ménage à trois*. Four hands, two tongues and two cocks. Instead of picturing her friend and two faceless men, she saw herself with Andre and Nathan. She imagined the two men touching her, caressing her. Each of them would kiss her, suck her nipples, play with her clit. One of them would fuck her pussy while the other one fucked her ass. She *really* wanted one of them to fuck her ass.

It would be *so* good.

Michelle glanced around the area. She had parked in the back of the restaurant. There was no street light above her, no one else nearby. Pushing back her seat, she unfastened her jeans and tugged them down her thighs so she could slide her hand inside her panties. She moaned when she touched her wet flesh.

Her clit was hard, begging for attention. Picking up the moisture from the feminine lips, Michelle spread it over her clit. She was so hot, she didn't need any build-up. Closing her eyes, she rubbed the swollen nub hard and fast.

The orgasm grabbed her in only moments. She pushed two fingers deep inside her channel and felt the walls contract around them.

Michelle slowly opened her eyes and blew out a deep breath. "Well, that was quick." She nervously glanced around again and breathed a sigh of relief when she didn't see anyone. After straightening her clothes, she started her car and backed out of the parking lot. She'd already had the climax. Another glass of wine and a long soak in the bathtub would be a perfect ending to the day.

Breanna's advice kept coming back to her as Michelle drove toward her house—"Don't think, just *do*." That was easy for her friend to say. While Michelle had no trouble going out with a guy and having a good time, she cringed when she thought of dating one of her escorts. They were her employees. She couldn't see how going out with someone who worked for her would be a good idea.

The ideal solution would be for her to meet a new man. She had dozens of girlfriends. Surely one of them had a brother or cousin or co-worker she could introduce to Michelle.

Michelle pulled into her garage. Not bothering with any lights, she stopped in the kitchen long enough to pour a glass of Pinot Grigio before making her way to the master bath off her bedroom. She lit several candles that were placed around the edge of the tub. Selecting lavender-scented bath salts, she poured them under the running water.

Michelle peeled off her clothes, stepped into the tub and relaxed beneath the mound of bubbles. Taking a sip of the cold wine, she smiled. Yes, that would be the ideal solution. A new man in her life would make her forget all about Andre and Nathan.

Chapter Five

ೲ

Nathan ran his tongue over Andre's balls and up the shaft. He slowly circled the head once, twice, before sliding back down.

"Oh, yeah." Andre lifted his hips from the bed. "Suck me."

"Don't bother me." He licked his lover's balls again. The musky scent of Andre's skin made his own balls tighten. "I'm busy here."

"Don't tease, Nathan."

"I like teasing." Pulling Andre's buttocks apart, he darted his tongue into his lover's ass. "I like making you crazy."

"You do a good job of it." He groaned when Nathan licked his anus. "*Jesus*, man!"

"You know you love it when I lick your ass."

"I do, but I'd love it better if you'd suck my dick."

"In a minute." Nathan pushed Andre's legs up until they touched Andre's chest. "Hold these. I want to play."

Andre hooked his hands behind his knees and spread his legs wide. Nathan touched the small puckered hole with the tip of his tongue. When Andre blew out a breath, Nathan pressed his tongue more firmly against Andre's anus. He licked all around the area before darting into Andre's ass.

"My God, I love that." Andre pulled his legs farther apart. "More. Fuck my ass with your tongue."

"You said you wanted me to suck your dick." He flicked the hole again. "Which do you want?"

"Both. Just make me come!"

"You're in too big a hurry. This is a suck and fuck day. Nice and slow, remember?"

"I'll slow down after I come." Andre dropped his legs to the bed. Grabbing his cock, he pushed it closer to Nathan's mouth. "Suck it."

"Well, if you insist…"

Nathan drew Andre's shaft into his mouth. He smiled to himself when Andre's body jerked. He knew how much Andre loved to have his cock sucked and licked…just as much as Nathan enjoyed doing it. He concentrated on the sensitive spot beneath the head, knowing that drove up Andre's desire as high as it could possibly go.

"*Damn*, Nathan. You are so good at that."

"Practice." Nathan tickled the slit with the tip of his tongue, savoring the flavor of Andre's pre-cum. "Lots of practice."

"Practice is good." He arched his hips, driving his cock deep into Nathan's mouth. "Oh, yeah, practice is *very* good."

Andre was close to coming and he wanted to come. Nathan knew that. He could keep up the slow loving, or drag it out even more and torture Andre a bit longer.

Nathan opted for the torture.

With one last lick over the head, Nathan released Andre's shaft. His lover didn't move for several seconds, then raised his head from the pillow and scowled at Nathan.

"What the hell? Why did you stop?"

Nathan rose to his knees between Andre's legs. "I wasn't ready for you to come."

"You weren't… Damn it, man, don't I get a say in this?"

"Nope." He leaned over and picked up a tube of lubricant from the nightstand. "I want to fuck you before you come."

A slow grin quirked Andre's lips. "Well, if you insist…"

Nathan spread the lube generously over his cock and Andre's anus. After wiping the excess from his hand, he grasped Andre's hips and tugged his lover's thighs on top of his. A shift of his pelvis and he buried himself to his balls.

"Mmm, yeah." Andre closed his eyes briefly. When he opened them again, Nathan clearly saw the heat in the green depths. "Feels so good."

Nathan pulled out until only the head remained inside Andre's ass, then thrust back inside. He could pump hard and fast and bring them both to shattering orgasms, but that wasn't what he wanted. He moved slowly, wanting to prolong the loving as long as possible.

"Love being inside you."

"Love you inside me."

Andre palmed his cock and started stroking it. Nathan watched for a moment. He liked to watch Andre touch himself, but he didn't want his lover to bring himself to orgasm that way. He pushed Andre's hand away. "Nuh-uh. No touching." He interlaced their fingers together. "Come just from me fucking you."

Taking Andre's other hand, Nathan leaned forward and pressed their hands into the pillow. He kissed Andre's lips as softly as he moved inside his lover. The kiss didn't stay soft. Andre nipped Nathan's bottom lip before driving his tongue deep into Nathan's mouth.

Groaning, Nathan opened his mouth wider and sucked on Andre's tongue. He was so lucky to have a lover who enjoyed kissing as much as he did. He kissed Andre again and again, then moved down to rain soft kisses over his neck and shoulder. A light sheen of perspiration made Andre's skin taste salty. The slow, easy thrusting continued as Nathan slid down to suck Andre's nipple. He pulled the tiny nub between his lips and flicked it with his tongue.

"Bite me," Andre whispered.

Clamping the nipple between his teeth, Nathan continued to flick it with his tongue. Andre moaned and bucked, but

Nathan refused to release his lover. He held Andre's hands still and played with his nipple while leisurely fucking him.

"Let me touch you," Andre rasped.

"No." Nathan raised up long enough to kiss Andre again, then returned to sucking his nipple. He knew Andre could break the hold if he wanted to. While not as husky as Nathan, Andre was every bit as strong. Instead he lay still, accepting the kisses, the nips, the thrusts.

Andre bucked again and moaned loudly. Nathan felt Andre's anus contract around his cock and a warm wetness against his skin. Lifting away from his lover, he saw Andre's cum on both their stomachs.

Seeing the evidence of Andre's orgasm heightened Nathan's own need for his release. Slow and easy was no longer an option. He pulled out of Andre's ass and fondled his own cock until his cum mixed with his lover's on Andre's stomach.

Andre smiled wickedly as he spread the creamy essence over his skin. "I liked that."

Nathan could barely breathe with his heart pounding so hard, but he managed to rasp, "Yeah, me too."

"It gets better every time, doesn't it?" Wiping a drop of cum from Nathan's slit, Andre licked it off his finger. "There's only one thing that could make it even better."

"Michelle."

"I want her, Nathan. I really want her."

"So do I." He stretched out beside Andre, leaning on one elbow. "We've been asking her out for almost two weeks. She keeps refusing."

"Then we keep asking. I'm not giving up. She's the one, Nathan. I feel it deep inside that she's the one."

Nathan caressed Andre's chest, stomach and softening cock. Although satisfied sexually—for now—Nathan still enjoyed touching Andre's skin. "I'll be gone for three days on that photo shoot in Houston. Maybe you can convince her to go out with you without me around."

"I have every intention of making love to her when she goes out with me. Would that be all right with you, if I have her without you there?"

Nathan nodded. "That might be better. You take her out, then I will. She needs to get to know each of us better before we tell her we're a couple. Of course, that all depends on whether or not you can charm her into bed. She could say no."

"She could, but I don't think she will. She reacts to us, Nathan…both of us." Andre chuckled. "We've taken out clients in the last two weeks, yet haven't had sex with any of them. Maybe we're losing our touch with women."

"Michelle said she'd set us up with women who usually wanted an escort with no sex involved to get us used to the job. I think that's what she's done." He continued to fondle Andre's cock. "Trust me, there's nothing lacking here. And you did get felt up by that bank president."

"True."

Nathan's fondling had the effect he wanted. Andre's shaft grew harder, longer, with each stroke of his fingers. "Looks like you're about ready for round two."

"Well, it is a suck and fuck day. There's supposed to be more than one round." Andre scooted closer to Nathan. "I have an idea."

"What?"

He slid his hand over Nathan's hip and between his buttocks to caress his anus. "Get me nice and hard again, and this time *I'll* fuck *you*."

Nathan smiled. "Works for me."

* * * * *

It was unusual for Michelle to see all of her escorts at one time. Not even on Mondays when she wrote out paychecks did all the guys arrive at once. They had regular daytime jobs, so usually straggled in at different times during the day or early evening to pick up their checks. The few times Brent or Zach had called a meeting, it had been on a Saturday or in the evening so everyone could be here. Brent had decided to call the meeting this evening. Rarely did any of the escorts work on Wednesday, so it was a good time for everyone to get together.

She sat on one of the stools at the bar and listened to her brother address the twenty-one men who worked for them. She looked at each one, studying their hair, their faces, their bodies. They ranged in age from twenty-five to forty-one. They were all handsome with great builds. None of them made her heart beat funny. No matter how good they looked, there wasn't one who made it difficult for her to breathe when she was near him.

Her gaze flashed to Andre, sitting on the stool to her right. Okay, there was one in the room who did it to her. If Nathan was here today, there would be two.

Andre winked at her before looking back at Brent. That simple gesture made her want to drag him into her office, push him down on her daybed and ravish him the rest of the night.

Maybe the rest of the week.

She blew out a breath and turned her attention back to her brother.

"Coopers' Companions has done extremely well the last two years," Brent said, "and we want to share that with y'all since we wouldn't be here without each one of you. Beginning Monday, your wages will increase fifty dollars for each date."

Brent's words were met with a round of applause. He smiled before continuing. "Now that summer vacations are over, we expect business to pick up even more. The holidays will be busy, of course. We've advertised for more escorts. You've all met Andre, our newest. Nathan's out of town, but most of you have met him too. Michelle hired them and I believe she did an excellent job."

More applause and whistles. Michelle tipped her head at the guys in thanks.

"Now I'm asking for help. We want to hire more escorts before the big holiday season. We'll continue to advertise, of course, but if y'all know of anyone who might be interested in working for us, tell him to come in for an interview."

"I have many cousins in Italy," Andre whispered into Michelle's ear. "Too bad they are not here."

His warm breath sent a shiver down her spine. It reminded her of the time in her office when he'd blown on her fingers. Michelle looked at him again. "Are they all as handsome as you?" she asked softly so no one else would hear her.

She groaned inwardly at her stupid question while Andre smiled. "I am pleased you find me handsome."

"What woman wouldn't?"

"Many."

"Then there's something wrong with them."

He smiled again. "I appreciate the compliment, but I only care about what *you* think of me."

She thought he was charming, funny, considerate...all qualities she desired in a man. Looks could fade over time. Passion might become a memory as a couple coped with the day-to-day problems of life. A companion, someone who would be there for her no matter what, meant more to her than a handsome face.

She felt strongly that Andre was that kind of man.

"Hey, Michelle," Brent said, "you want to pay attention?"

Michelle whipped her head back toward her brother. Warmth filled her cheeks and traveled down into her neck, but she raised her chin. There was no way she'd let her brother know he had embarrassed her. "Say something interesting and I'll listen."

The guys laughed while Brent frowned at her. Grinning, she licked her finger and raised it in the air. Brent's frown faded. He laughed while shaking his head.

"Thank God I only have one sister. Okay, I guess that wraps it up. Thanks for coming."

Some of the escorts rose as if to leave. Some remained in their chairs as if they would stay a while and visit. Michelle slid off her stool, rounded the bar and walked into the kitchen to refill her iced tea glass. Andre followed closely behind her.

"I did not expect a raise so soon."

"Business has been good. We believe in sharing the wealth with our escorts."

"Have dinner with me."

The abrupt change of subject threw her. She set her glass on the counter and looked up into Andre's face. She'd been putting him and Nathan off for almost two weeks because of her rule about not dating the escorts. They hadn't given up, despite her saying no repeatedly. Now, standing here looking into Andre's intense green eyes, her rule no longer seemed to matter. "I'd like that."

His eyes widened in surprise. "You will dine with me?"

She nodded. "I will."

Smiling, he reached over and squeezed her arm. "Not tonight. I wish to take you somewhere very special. Tomorrow evening?"

"All right."

"I will need your address so I can pick you up."

"I can meet you—"

"No." Andre slid his fingers down her arm and took her hand. "A gentleman picks up his lady and sees her home."

Michelle had another rule—always meet the guy when it's a first date instead of telling him where she lived. She lived outside the city in a quiet subdivision. Telling a man her address before she knew him would be incredibly stupid. That rule didn't apply with Andre. She already knew him, and she trusted him. "I'll write down my address and directions for you."

* * * * *

Brent leaned back in his chair and laced his fingers behind his head. "You and Andre looked very chummy during the meeting."

Michelle glanced up from her keyboard at her brother. His casual posture didn't fool her. He had something on his mind and was waiting for the right time to spring it on her. "No more chummy than with any of the other guys."

"You didn't sit by any of the other guys."

Ignoring him, she selected a column on her spreadsheet and pressed the necessary keystrokes for a total. "You know, we could go up seventy-five on the wages and still do great."

"Zach suggested fifty. You and I agreed. It's good for now."

"Then we'll give bigger Christmas bonuses. If things keep going as well as they have, we can do that easily."

"Are you dating Andre?"

Brent had never learned the art of subtlety. Giving up on her work for now, Michelle saved her file and turned her chair to face her brother. "I wasn't."

"Meaning you are now?"

"We're having dinner tomorrow night."

"I don't think that's a good idea."

"I don't remember asking your permission."

"Michelle." He leaned forward in his chair and braced his elbows on his knees. "When I said it would be a good idea for you to date some of the escorts, I meant the ones we've known

63

for a while. Andre's been here two weeks. Don't you think you should get to know him better before you go out with him?"

"Are you forgetting you told me last week that I should go out with one of the new guys? Your exact words, Brent. Besides, dinner is a good way to get to know someone."

"What about Peter? He's crazy about you."

"I'm not crazy about him."

"Okay, so how about—"

"Brent, this isn't open to discussion. I don't tell you who to date. You have no right to tell me who to date."

He frowned. "I'm only thinking of you."

"No, you're trying to run my life, just like you've always done."

He opened his mouth as if to speak again, but Michelle quickly continued before he could. "Brent, you're my brother and I love you, but you're too controlling. You have to dip your fingers into everything around you. That doesn't work with me. It never has and it never will.

His frown deepened. "I don't try to run your life."

"Yes, you do. But I know that and I won't let it influence what I do. Andre has been asking me out since I met him. I kept saying no, then I decided it's stupid for me to refuse when I want to get to know him better. I feel something strong for him, Brent. I need to find out exactly what that is."

He looked at her for several moments without speaking. Then he sighed and leaned back in his chair. "Okay. If you want to date Andre, I won't say another word about it. I promise."

"Thank you."

"I only want what's best for you. You know that, right?"

Michelle smiled. Her brother might be domineering and bossy, but she knew he loved her. "Yes, I know that. And don't worry. I know exactly what I'm doing."

* * * * *

Michelle had no idea what she was doing.

Andre had said he wanted to take her somewhere special. She didn't know what he considered "special", so had no idea what to wear. She'd already discarded five dresses that weren't quite right. He'd be here in less than an hour and she still didn't know what to wear.

She wanted to look beautiful and alluring. And sexy. That wouldn't be easy since she didn't consider herself sexy. Attractive, yes. Attractive wasn't sexy. Attractive didn't make a man's tongue hang out when she walked by.

She wanted to be sexy for Andre.

Michelle chewed on her thumbnail while she studied the contents of her closet. Nothing jumped out at her. Nothing seemed right to wear on her first…

She sucked in a sharp breath when she remembered the blue dress.

Moving to the back of her walk-in closet, Michelle located a padded hanger covered by a plastic bag. The dress beneath the plastic had been Breanna's idea. Michelle had gone along with buying something she wouldn't normally buy because her friend had talked her into it. It had hung in her closet for two months, ever since she'd purchased it off the sale rack at Dillard's.

Michelle carried the hanger to her bed. Removing the plastic, she held up the dress and examined it. A rich royal blue, it had tiny spaghetti straps, a deep scooped neck and an even deeper back. The soft, flowing fabric hugged her curves all the way to just above her knees.

Biting her lower lip, Michelle wondered if she had the nerve to wear the scrap of material. The low cut in the front and a nonexistent back made wearing a bra impossible.

This would be the perfect dress if she wanted to look sexy.

A slow smile turned up Michelle's lips. *Why not? I'm feeling daring tonight.*

Her decision made, Michelle removed her silky robe and tossed it on the bed. Searching through her underwear drawer, she picked out the smallest pair of panties she owned. A black wisp of nylon and lace, the thong barely covered her pubic hair. Sheer black thigh-high stockings and strappy black heels would complete the outfit.

Wearing only the thong, Michelle sat at her dresser to put on her makeup. She sorted through her eye shadows until she found the perfect one. Opening the case, she removed the brush and leaned forward to apply the shadow to her lids. Instead of looking at her face, her gaze dipped to her bare breasts. Large and firm, they'd always drawn a lot of attention from men. David had loved them. He'd especially loved covering them with lube and sliding his cock between them until he came.

She wondered if Andre liked large breasts.

They'd make love tonight. Michelle had no doubt about that. He wouldn't have been so insistent about their dating if he didn't want her.

She definitely wanted him.

Michelle cradled her breasts and thumbed her nipples. She moaned softly when her womb contracted and her clit tingled. It was tempting to slide her hand inside her thong and bring herself to a climax. As hot as she felt, it wouldn't take long.

No. She didn't want to come with her own hand. She'd been doing that ever since David broke up with her. The next time she came, it would be with a man's tongue licking her clit or with his cock buried deep inside her pussy.

It would be Andre's tongue, Andre's cock.

Michelle shivered. Giving her nipples one more gentle pinch that made her breath catch, she reached for her eye shadow again.

* * * * *

Andre had thought Michelle lovely the first time he saw her. That knowledge didn't prepare him for the vision who answered the door.

He noticed her hair first. She'd swept it up on top of her head with curls hanging down her neck. A pair of diamond studs glittered in her lobes. Her eyes looked huge from liner and mascara, her lips shiny from a deep wine-colored lipstick. His gaze continued downward, stopping at her breasts. They almost spilled out of the neckline of her dress.

He clenched his fists to keep from reaching out and cradling them in his hands.

His gaze continued downward, taking in her womanly hips and shapely legs. He looked at the sexy high-heeled sandals on her feet before making the return journey up her body to her face.

"Hi," she said softly.

"Good evening." He glanced at her breasts one more time. "*Mi lasci senza fiato.*"

Her brows drew together. "What does that mean?"

Andre took her hand, lifted it to his mouth and kissed the back. "It means you leave me breathless."

"Oh," she said weakly.

Smiling to himself, Andre kissed her hand again. "May I come in?"

"Yes. Of course. Please."

She moved aside and Andre stepped into her foyer. He saw the living room to his left and the dining room to his right. He assumed the short hall in front of him led to the bedrooms.

"You have a lovely home."

"Thank you. My uncle and brothers built it last year."

"May I have a tour?"

"Do we have time?"

Andre glanced at his watch. "Our reservation is at seven-thirty. We are twenty minutes from the restaurant."

Michelle smiled. "Then follow me."

Anywhere, Andre thought.

She led him into the living room first. Andre watched the gentle sway of her hips beneath the clinging blue dress. The low-cut back dipped almost to those sexy rounded buttocks. A dress cut that low in both front and back wouldn't let her wear a bra.

He wondered if she'd decided to forgo panties too.

Focusing on the furnishings of Michelle's house instead of her body, he examined the décor as they walked through the living room. He wasn't familiar with the different styles of furniture like Nathan, but he recognized antiques. Michelle had used soft neutrals mixed with bold jewel tones in the color scheme. The décor wasn't overly feminine, but comfortable and inviting. It fit her perfectly.

An open doorway led into the hall. She showed him the two extra bedrooms, one of which she'd turned into her office. He saw the main bathroom next, then she started to lead him away from the room at the end of the hall.

"Wait." He motioned toward the closed door. "What room is that?"

She clasped her hands together. "My bedroom."

"Is it off limits?"

"Not off limits, just…messy. I tend to ignore it and shut the door."

"The fastest way to clean a room is to shut the door. Nathan taught me that."

Michelle laughed. "He's very clever."

"I am a bit neater than Nathan, but sometimes I will let things…slide? Is that the right word?"

"Yes, that's the right word."

Taking her hand, he lightly squeezed her fingers. "Perhaps you will show me your bedroom another time."

She hitched in a breath. "Perhaps," she whispered.

He smiled at her reaction to his touch. Or perhaps she was reacting to the thought of sharing her bed with him.

He hoped it was the latter.

Following her once again, they returned to the living room. Andre draped the soft shawl of black silk around Michelle's shoulders as she picked up her small purse from the end table by the couch. Leaning forward, he dropped a gentle kiss on her neck.

"You are so lovely."

She turned to face him. Desire clearly showed in her eyes. If he took her hand again and tugged her down the hall to that closed door, he had no doubt she'd open it for him.

Not yet. He wanted this evening to be special for her. There would be dining, dancing and getting to know each other better before they shared their bodies. He wanted to show her how good they could be together...in every way.

Chapter Six

໑

Michelle couldn't believe it when Andre pulled into the parking lot of Paul's Garden. One of the newer restaurant in the Metroplex, it had quickly garnered a reputation for incredible food and service. She'd wanted to eat here ever since it opened. "You made a reservation *here*?"

"Yes." He turned off the ignition and faced her. "You do not like Italian food?"

"I *love* it. But this place has a waiting list for reservations. How did you get one so quickly?"

He brushed her cheek with his thumb. "I talked to the owner and told him I planned to dine with a special lady. He was happy to help."

He cradled her cheek in his palm. He watched the movement of his thumb as he rubbed it back and forth across her mouth. Michelle parted her lips slightly in preparation for his kiss.

Instead of kissing her as she expected, he looked into her eyes and gave her a gentle smile. "Shall we go in?"

She'd rather stay in the car and make out. She wanted to slide the tie from around Andre's neck, unbutton that snowy white shirt, see if his chest was as gorgeous as she'd envisioned. It would be bare, or perhaps have a sprinkling of hair down the center. The muscles would be sculptured, the nipples small and brown. She knew many men had nipples just as sensitive as a woman's and received a great deal of pleasure when they were licked and sucked. She could see herself licking one of those small nubs, then the other one, before dragging her tongue down his stomach to the prize inside his pants…

The sound of her door opening jerked her back to the present. Andre stood by the open door, offering her his hand. Picking up her clutch from the floor, she placed her hand in his.

The interior of the restaurant was every bit as elegant as Michelle had suspected. A gracious hostess showed her and Andre to a private, secluded table at the back of the restaurant. Andre held Michelle's chair for her before taking the one opposite. With a smile, the hostess handed them menus, then disappeared.

A large window to her right drew Michelle's attention. Flowers and shrubs gave her the feeling of actually dining in a garden.

"The flowers are lovely, yes?"

Michelle looked back at Andre. "Yes, they are."

"It reminds me of my family's home. My mother has a beautiful garden. It is her pride and joy."

She hadn't spoken with Andre about his life before he moved to America. "Your parents are still in Italy?"

"Yes. I come from the region of Veneto near Verona."

"Verona. Isn't that where Romeo and Juliet lived? Or supposedly lived."

Andre nodded. "You know your Shakespeare."

"Let's not go that far. I can't tell you anything about *Macbeth* or *Othello*." She leaned forward. "Tell me more about your home."

"I will tell you anything you wish to know, but we should decide on our meal first."

She'd forgotten all about food when he began talking of Italy. She wanted to learn more about him, to hear about his life before they met. She'd listen to anything he said simply to hear that sexy accent.

Once the waiter had taken their order, Michelle leaned forward again and rested her arms on the table. "Okay, so tell me all about your home."

"I would like to hear about *your* life."

"My life is boring."

"I do not think anything about you could be boring."

His intense gaze made her heart beat a bit faster. "That's very sweet, but I'd really like to hear about you."

The waiter returned with their wine and poured a small amount into Andre's glass. Andre nodded his approval after taking a sip.

"Very good."

He didn't speak again until the waiter had filled their wineglasses and left. Picking up his glass, he held it toward Michelle. "I offer a toast to my dinner companion. May this be the first of many evenings together."

Michelle clinked her wineglass against his. She sipped the deep red wine, enjoying the bite on her tongue as she swallowed. "Mmm, this *is* good."

"My family has owned a vineyard for generations. We produce a dry white wine called Soave. It is very popular in our region."

"Did you work in the vineyard?"

Andre nodded. "I have three brothers. My father had all of us work in the vineyards as well as the winery."

"Did you enjoy it?"

"I did, but it did not take me long to realize it was not what I wanted to do with my life."

Michelle swirled the wine in her glass. "I doubt if you dreamed of being an escort."

"No," Andre said with a chuckle.

He said nothing further. After taking a sip of wine, she set her glass back on the table. "So what did you want to do with your life?"

"I wanted to write."

"Write? You mean novels?"

"Mystery novels, to be exact. They have always been my passion. I have loved to read since I was a small boy."

"Are you any good?"

He gave her a cocky grin that totally charmed her. "Yes."

Michelle laughed. "Do you have a book published?"

"No. I have an agent who is sending out my manuscript to publishers." He shrugged one shoulder. "The odds are high, but perhaps someday."

"Are you writing another book?"

"Yes."

"May I read it?"

Andre shook his head. "Not until it is finished."

"What about the first one, the one your agent is sending out? May I read it?"

That cocky little grin turned up his lips again. "Perhaps we can work out a…deal."

If his idea of a "deal" included massage oil and naked skin, she'd make that deal right now.

Until then, Michelle wanted him to keep talking in that bone-melting accent. She picked up her wineglass and held it in both hands. "Tell me more about growing up in Italy."

*   *   *   *   *

Andre held Michelle's hand as they strolled toward her front door. He moved as slowly as possible, in no hurry to see the evening end.

She'd enjoyed their time together. He didn't doubt that. Conversation had flowed easily between them. Dinner had been superb. They'd had more wine with their meal, then rich coffee and lemon cheesecake for dessert. Michelle had claimed she wouldn't be able to move for at least three days after eating so much. She'd changed her mind when he'd asked her to dance.

Holding her in his arms while they moved to the romantic music made him long for more. He wanted to make love to her, but it was more than that. He couldn't remember ever feeling so close to a woman. He truly believed she was the one who would complete him.

So did Nathan. Andre had talked to him on the phone this afternoon. His partner had been happy when Andre told him about the date with Michelle. Nathan had also been jealous. He'd said he wanted full details when he got back from Houston, and that it would be his turn to date Michelle.

Then, they would have her at the same time.

Blood rushed to Andre's cock at the thought of Michelle spread out on her bed, sucking his shaft while Nathan licked her pussy. He'd play with those gorgeous breasts as his lover pushed two fingers up her ass. Andre would be on the verge of a climax before he pulled out of her mouth and switched places with Nathan.

He could hardly wait to taste her.

At the front door, Michelle released his hand and opened her purse. When she withdrew her ring of keys, he took it from her. "Which one?"

Silently, she pointed to a brass one with a blue plastic ring around the head. Andre unlocked the door and pushed it open, then stood back so she could enter the house first. This is where she would either invite him in, or say goodnight.

Once past the threshold, she faced him again. "Would you like a glass of wine? Or I can make coffee."

Andre stepped inside and shut the door behind him. Looking into her eyes, he lifted one hand and traced the neckline of her dress with his fingertips. "The only thing I want is you."

* * * * *

Michelle had anticipated this all evening. Now that she and Andre were close to making love, nerves tightened her stomach.

She wasn't a stranger to physical love. Several men had made love to her since that first groping session with Billy Hamden in the backseat of his father's car when she was seventeen. He hadn't a clue how to treat a girl, nor had he cared about that. He'd wanted to get off, so she'd brought him to a climax with her hand in less than a minute. That's when she'd realized *she* was in charge, not the boy. She was the one responsible for her pleasure, no one else. If her lover didn't please her, she took care of herself.

Standing here, looking into Andre's emerald gaze, Michelle had no doubt that there would be no need for her to take care of herself tonight.

He slid one hand around her neck. "I want to make love to you."

Unable to speak with desire clogging her throat, Michelle nodded.

"You have many candles in your home. Are they in your bedroom too?"

"Yes," she whispered.

"Go light them. Do not turn on a lamp." He squeezed her neck. "I will get us some wine."

Her legs trembled as she walked down the hall to her bedroom. Desire coursed through her veins, hot and thick. Her panties were already damp, and Andre had barely touched her.

In her bedroom, Michelle quickly scooped up her robe and the dresses she'd decided not to wear from the bed and tossed them in the closet, along with her wrap and purse. She hurriedly straightened the bedspread, thankful she'd changed her sheets today. She'd also filled all the candleholders with spiced vanilla votives and pillars. As per Andre's instruction, she took a long lighter from the nightstand drawer and circled the room, touching the flame to each wick. She'd lit the last one when she heard her door open.

Andre stood in the doorway, holding a glass of wine in each hand. He'd taken off his jacket and removed his tie. The top three buttons of his shirt were open, giving her an enticing glimpse of smooth tan skin.

It would be horribly unladylike to attack him, but that's exactly what she wanted to do.

He held out a glass toward her. "I found this nice Chardonnay in your refrigerator."

It could be vinegar and she wouldn't care. "I don't know as much about wine as you do. I buy what I like."

"You have excellent taste." He sipped the cold liquid, watching her over the rim of the glass. His gaze dipped to her breasts. "In wine and dresses."

"I wanted to look sexy for you."

"You succeeded." He took a step closer to her. "Sexy and beautiful."

He kissed her, softly, gently, barely brushing her lips with his. The hint of wine flavored his breath. Michelle clutched her wineglass with both hands to keep from grabbing him. She couldn't remember ever feeling this hot, this needy, for a man.

She parted her lips for his tongue. He slid it along the seam, dabbed it at the corners, but didn't enter her mouth. Instead, he sipped at her lips again and again, taking his time seducing her.

Ohmigod, does this man know how to kiss!

A soft moan escaped from her throat. Andre lifted his head. A teasing light filled his eyes. "Do you like that?"

"What's not to like? But you…" Michelle stopped, unsure how to tell him to *take* her.

"But I what?"

She gasped when he dipped one finger into her cleavage. "I've already said yes. You don't have to seduce me."

"Ah, but seducing is very nice." He moved his fingertip to her left nipple. "I like to take my time and give my partner much pleasure."

Michelle moaned again when he lightly pinched her nipple between his thumb and forefinger. As if in apology for possibly hurting her, he rubbed the nub with the pad of his thumb. "Do you like a man to play with your nipples?"

"Yes. Oh, yes."

"Lick them?"

"Yes."

"Suck them?"

"You're killing me here, Andre."

He chuckled, low and wicked. Slipping his hand into the bodice of her dress, he palmed her breast. "I am trying to prepare you for me."

"I'm ready, trust me."

"Are you?" He continued to caress her breast as he looked into her eyes. "Is your pussy wet?"

The graphic question coming from a man who had shown her nothing but tenderness and consideration surprised her…and made her clit throb. She nodded.

Andre set his wineglass on her dresser. "Show me."

She blinked at his unexpected demand. "What?"

"Show me." He sat on the end of her bed, knees spread wide, and braced his fists on the bed. "I want to see if you're wet."

His position clearly showed her the large bulge in his pants. Their love play was obviously affecting him. Surely he didn't expect a striptease on their first date.

Then again, why not?

Michelle set her glass next to his on the dresser. When she turned back to him, she saw the heat in his eyes. They glowed like emeralds in the candlelight.

"Show me," Andre whispered.

He swallowed when Michelle began to slowly move her hips from side to side, as if she heard a song inside her mind. Closing her eyes, she ran her hands over her breasts, her stomach, her thighs. Andre didn't think his cock could possibly get any harder. Seeing Michelle move so freely, so provocatively, caused all the blood in his body to rush into his shaft. He couldn't think. He couldn't move. All he could do was stare at her and enjoy her show.

She circled her hips as she turned her back to him. Her hands drifted over her buttocks, tugging up her dress a few inches so he could see the back of her thighs. She wore dark stockings with lace around the top. He caught a glimpse of skin above the stockings before she lowered the dress again. Lifting her hands to her head, she unfastened the clip holding her hair. It tumbled past her shoulders in a chestnut wave.

He wanted to bury his hands in it while feasting on her mouth.

Andre shifted on the bed, hoping to relieve some of the pressure on his cock. Michelle's hips kept moving in a slow circle. Each movement made her dress ride up and down her thighs. Each movement gave him that tiny glimpse of lace and skin.

The dress crept up and up until he could see the beginning curves of her ass. The teasing was incredibly sexy, but he didn't know how much more he could take before he grabbed her and threw her on the bed. He wanted to go slow, make it good for her, but a man could only take so much before he had to be in control.

His breath hitched when she pulled up her dress to her waist.

"My God," he muttered.

A tiny piece of dark fabric divided those round buttocks. Unable to resist touching her any longer, Andre cradled her cheeks in his palms. Squeezing and pulling them apart, he ran one thumb up and down the crevice.

"Bend over."

She did as he said, clasping her knees. Hooking his thumbs in the thong, he slowly slid it over her buttocks and down her legs.

"Step out of it."

Again, she did as he said with no hesitation. Andre liked that. She bent over again without him telling her. Her hot, musky scent drifted to his nose. Leaning closer to her, he inhaled deeply. It'd been much too long since he'd enjoyed the aroma of an aroused woman.

Or the taste.

Andre parted her labia and swiped his tongue across her moist flesh. "Mmm, you *are* wet."

"To-told you."

Her breathless answer made him smile. "Does this mean you want me?"

"Very much."

He licked her swollen flesh again. "What do you want me to do?"

"Everything."

"Mmm, sounds promising." Slipping his hands between her thighs, he pushed outward until Michelle widened her stance another few inches. "That is better. Pull your cheeks apart so I can see this sweet pussy."

Andre waited until she'd obeyed his command before touching her again. Using only one forefinger, he slid it over the wet, swollen flesh until he reached her clit. Already hard, it grew even larger as he rubbed it. Andre planned to drive his tongue as far inside her as he could. But first, he wanted to make her come on his hand.

"Tell me what you need, *amore mia*. Tell me how to touch you."

"Just-just like that." She arched her back. "Oh, yes, that's good."

There was so much passion inside her, just as Andre suspected. Taking his time, driving up her desire slowly, wouldn't be easy when he wanted to bury his shaft inside her and fuck her until neither of them could move.

Andre's fingers slid over her feminine lips, his path made easy by her juices. Her breathing became deeper, heavier. She dropped her head and pushed her buttocks back at him.

"There. Right there."

Suspecting she was close to a climax, he pushed two fingers into her pussy. The contractions deep inside her grabbed his fingers. She moaned, trembled, then stilled.

Michelle blew out her breath. *Wow*, she thought. It was a good thing she'd locked her knees or she'd be a pile on the floor right now. She knew how to touch herself to make her come quickly. Having an orgasm so fast with a man was unusual. Even the most talented lover needed time to learn her body, learn what pleased her.

Andre was most definitely a talented lover.

The gentle nip of Andre's teeth on her buttock made her smile. "You're a dangerous man, Andre D'Amato."

"I am a man who appreciates a sexy woman."

She turned to face him. Tunneling her fingers into his thick hair, she bent over and kissed him deeply. "Thank you. For the orgasm and the compliment."

Andre smiled. "My pleasure." He squeezed her buttocks. "Are you ready for round two?"

A laugh bubbled from her mouth. "Round two? I can't breathe now."

"You do not have to breathe. You only have to feel."

A tug on her wrist had her tumbling on top of him, one leg on either side of his. Sliding his hands over her bare bottom, he lifted his hips and pressed his erection into her mound. "Hello there."

Michelle laughed again. "Hi."

"I hope you do not think we are through."

"Uh, no." She shifted on top of him, driving his hard cock farther between her legs. "It feels like we won't be through for a while."

"Make that a *long* while."

The next instant, Michelle found herself on her back with Andre leaning over her. He tugged her into a sitting position long enough to pull the dress over her head and toss it to the floor. Cradling the back of her head, he kissed her while lowering her to the bed. His free hand moved over her breasts, her stomach, between her legs.

She thought it incredibly sexy for Andre to be fully clothed while she wore only her stockings and sandals.

Andre removed her shoes and tossed them to the floor with her dress. Moving between her legs, he pressed on her knees until she spread them wide, her feet planted on the bed. He stared at her pussy while unbuttoning his shirt.

"You shave."

Michelle touched the soft tuft of hair on her mound. "Just the lips. I don't shave here."

"It is very sexy."

His shirt joined her clothing on the floor. Michelle inhaled sharply at the sight of all that tan skin and sculptured muscles.

Andre's chest was bare, the only hair a small strip that flowed downward from his navel.

Breanna called that the happy trail. It would make Michelle very happy to follow that trail with her tongue.

He slowly rolled her stockings down her legs and tossed them to the floor. He kissed her left knee, then her right. Soft nips with his teeth made Michelle squirm on the bed as her clit throbbed. She wanted to see all of Andre, not just his chest.

"Take off your pants."

He ran his tongue up the inside of her thigh. "In time."

"I want to see you."

"I want to make you come with my tongue."

He sucked on the soft skin at the crease of her leg. Michelle had the fleeting thought that she'd have a hickey there tomorrow. All thought ceased when he ran his tongue over her labia. Closing her eyes, she concentrated on the sensation of Andre's tongue on her flesh. He licked up and down the feminine lips, but didn't touch her clit.

"*Delizioso.*"

Michelle wasn't sure what that meant, and right now she didn't care. Grabbing handfuls of Andre's hair, she tried to guide his tongue to the aching nub.

"There. Lick me there."

"Here?" He barely touched her clit with the tip of his tongue.

"Yes. Mmm, that's good."

"What if I do this?" He drove his tongue inside her channel. "Or maybe this?" His tongue darted into her ass.

"*Oh, God!*"

Michelle lifted her hips, trying to get that wicked tongue closer to her anus. She loved to feel the rasp of a man's tongue across that sensitive area.

Her action must have spurred something inside Andre. No longer teasing, he now ran his tongue up and down her intimate flesh in an erotic dance that stole the breath from her lungs. Stretching her arms over her head, she arched her back and raised her hips another few inches. There. Right there. A bit more time with that talented tongue on her clit and she'd be flying.

The orgasm almost blew off the top of her head. Michelle released a keening moan as the pleasure rushed through her body.

Small tremors raced over her. When the last one died, she opened her eyes. Andre straddled her body on his hands and knees, his eyes dark and burning with heat.

"Unfasten my pants."

Easy for him to say. Michelle didn't know if she could get her fingers to work. She took a breath and blew it out before reaching for Andre's belt. It took her two tries to unfasten it.

He chuckled. "Having problems?"

"Yes, and don't sound so smug about it." She loosened the button. "I'm trying to remember how to think."

He kissed her softly. "I am pleased to make you feel so deeply."

His kiss made her lose her train of thought again. She didn't understand how he could make it to the age of thirty-one without a woman chaining him to her bed and refusing to let him go.

Andre kissed her lips, her chin, her neck. He liked knowing their lovemaking affected her so strongly. It wouldn't if she didn't feel more for him than simple desire. "Michelle. My pants."

"Pants. Right." She lowered the zipper and tugged his pants past his hips. Her eyes widened. "No underwear?"

"No."

Her gaze shot up to his. "Just tonight, or ever?"

"I do not like underwear."

She groaned softly. "Oh, God, that's hot."

"*You* are hot." He kissed her deeply, driving his tongue past her lips. "Touch me, *cara mia.*"

Her fingers slid up and down his shaft. Andre closed his eyes. She cradled his balls with one hand and caressed the head with the other. Her hands were magical. "Yes, that is the way. Touch me." He moved his hips, slowly pumping his cock through her fingers. "I could come this way."

"Do it," she whispered.

"I wish to be inside you."

"You can do that later. Please. I want to watch you come."

Andre moved his hips faster as he stared into Michelle's luminous eyes. She tightened her fingers around his shaft. Pleasure gripped his balls, galloped down his spine. With a groan, he shot his cum on the soft skin of her stomach and breasts.

Michelle was right. Forming a coherent thought after such a powerful orgasm was impossible. His arms and legs trembled. He had to concentrate to keep them straight so he didn't fall on top of Michelle.

Although lying on top of her didn't sound like a bad idea.

She ran one finger through his essence on her breast. "Good one, huh?"

He laughed. "Yes, it was a good one."

Lifting her finger to her mouth, she swiped off the drop with her tongue. Andre sat back on his heels and watched her scoop up another drop and lick it off her finger.

"You taste good."

He circled her clit with his thumb. "So do you." With his free hand, he spread his seed over her stomach and breasts, paying special attention to her nipples. "Do you want a washcloth?"

She shook her head. "I want you to hold me."

"Gladly."

Andre rose from the bed. While he removed his shoes, socks and pants, Michelle drew back the covers and slipped between the sheets. He soon joined her, taking her in his arms and pulling her close to his side.

It felt right to hold her.

"I have to blow out the candles," she said, running her hand over his chest.

"Not yet." He cradled her cheek in his hand. "You look beautiful in the candlelight."

She smiled. "Thank you."

"Besides, I have every intention of making love to you again."

"Oh, really?"

"I haven't been inside that delicious pussy yet."

"Oh. Well, I certainly wouldn't want to spoil your fun."

Chapter Seven

∽

He kissed her slowly, his tongue tracing her lips, her teeth. Michelle sighed and melted back into her pillow. It'd been a long time since a man's kiss stirred her so deeply. It'd been a long time since she'd had two such powerful orgasms and still wanted more.

The feel of Andre's hardening cock pressed to her thigh proved he wanted more too.

He plucked at her nipple as he kissed her. Michelle arched her back, lifting her breast closer to his hand.

"What do you need?" he asked against her lips.

"Suck my nipples."

He drew one hard nipple between his lips. Michelle tunneled her fingers into his hair when he began to suckle. Each tug of his lips made her womb contract.

Something that felt this good must be illegal in several states.

"I love your breasts." Andre squeezed her generous flesh as he switched to the other nipple. "So big and firm." He nipped the nub with his teeth. "Beautiful." He slid one hand down her stomach to between her thighs. "You are beautiful everywhere."

He kissed her again as he moved between her legs. Sliding his hands beneath her buttocks, he lifted her hips in preparation to enter her. The tip of his cock brushed her labia.

"Do you use birth control?"

She nodded. "I'm on the Pill."

"You have seen my blood work. You know I am clean. Do you wish me to wear a condom?"

She touched his hair, his face, his shoulders. Grasping his waist, she raised her hips so the head of his shaft slipped inside her. "I don't want anything to separate us."

At that moment, he knew he loved her.

Andre pushed forward, filling her heat. The tight walls of her pussy closed around his cock. He moaned when he felt those walls squeeze his hard flesh.

"Michelle," he rasped.

A wicked feminine smile touched her lips. "Like that?"

"Do it again."

Her internal muscles squeezed his cock once more. He moved forward, back, forward again, slowly picking up the rhythm. Her fingernails dug into his buttocks as she met each thrust. Andre wanted to look into her eyes as he fucked her, but he wanted to hold her more. Gathering her in his arms, he dropped soft kisses on her neck and shoulder while he moved inside her.

Her soft breath tickled his ear before he felt the bite of her teeth on the lobe. So his lady wanted to play a bit rougher. Andre slid his arms beneath her knees and spread them wider. His thrusts became faster, harder, until the pounding rocked her bed as well as her body.

"Mmm, *yes*!" Andre sucked on Michelle's neck as the orgasm ripped through him. He thrust again and again into her channel while the powerful sensation trickled down to a warm glow.

It took him several moments to realize Michelle hadn't experienced the intense feelings he had. He kissed her neck in apology. "I am sorry."

Her hands glided up and down his spine. "For what?"

He lifted his head and looked into her eyes. "I was too fast. You did not come again."

"I came twice. Trust me, I'm happy." She ran her fingernails lightly over his buttocks. "It's hard for me to come in this position."

"Which position do you prefer?"

"On top."

"Ah, so you like to be in charge."

She grinned. "Sure."

Andre chuckled. "I will remember that next time."

"Next time?" Andre winced when she pinched his cheek. "Who said there would be a next time?"

He loved the teasing light in her eyes. "I am hoping there will be many times like this."

She touched his chin, his lips, her fingertips grazing his skin. "That would be nice."

A declaration of love would be too soon. Andre knew that. Still, he had to show her how he felt about her. He kissed her deeply, pouring all the love in his heart into his kiss. She answered in kind, her tongue darting over his lips and into his mouth.

The need to breathe made Andre end the kiss long before he wanted to. Panting for breath, he rested his forehead against hers. "I could quickly become addicted to your kisses."

"Mmm, me too. About yours."

He kissed her once more, a bare brush of his lips to hers. "May I spend the night?"

Michelle smiled. "I'd like that."

* * * * *

It's amazing how good a person can feel after a night of great sex.

Michelle sighed in satisfaction as she opened her spreadsheet program. Work was the last thing she wanted to do today, but she had several items to post. She liked to keep on top of her paperwork so she could generate her guys' paychecks first thing Monday morning.

Leaving Andre this morning and coming into the office hadn't been easy. She wished she could've prepared breakfast for them, spent time with him in her sunny breakfast nook. She always took off Tuesday and Wednesday, and any other day she could manage to squeeze out of Brent and Zach. Maybe she should invite him over for dinner Monday night. Then she could get up on Tuesday and cook a fabulous, huge brunch. Well, at least scrambled eggs and English muffins. Michelle was the first to admit cooking wasn't one of her better talents. After brunch, she would spend the rest of the day making love with the sexy Italian.

She sighed again. Oh, yes, she liked that idea very much.

The phone rang. With one hand still on the computer keys, Michelle reached for the receiver. "Coopers' Companions, this is Michelle."

"Hello, Michelle. This is Angela Dubois."

The gorgeous blonde didn't have to identify herself. Michelle knew that sultry voice as soon as Angela said hello. Michelle had met Angela only once, but that one time was enough to leave a lasting impression. The woman sent out a strong signal that said "fuck me." Single and filthy rich from a large inheritance, she liked to party as often as possible.

Her partying included systematically going through every one of Coopers' Companions' escorts.

"Good morning, Ms. Dubois. How can I help you?"

"I'm having a small get-together at my penthouse tonight. I'd like one of your escorts to be my date."

Michelle never asked her guys about their dates. Anything personal that happened between them and their dates was none of her business. Being guys and considering her the same as a little sister, sometimes they volunteered information about the women they escorted. Most of them had already been out with Angela Dubois. All of those dates included sex.

She could be very…persuasive. And extremely easy.

"I'm sure I can help you. Just a moment."

Switching screens on the computer, Michelle brought up the appointment schedule. Only three of her guys were free tonight. "I can send Peter. He would be happy to be your date."

Angela sighed heavily. "No, not Peter. He's handsome and charming, but I've already dated him. I want someone new, someone different."

"How about Reese?"

"I've dated him too. Don't you have someone totally new?"

It took all her willpower not to shoot Angela a raspberry over the phone. Michelle stared at the remaining name on the schedule—Andre. She couldn't send Andre on a date with this barracuda, not after spending the night in his arms.

You have to. It's his job.

She cleared her throat. "Actually, I do have two new escorts. One is in Houston until Sunday, but Andre is available."

"Andre?" Michelle could imagine Angela's eyebrows disappearing into her bangs at the thought of new blood. "Is he foreign?"

"Italian."

"My God. Gorgeous, dark hair, dark eyes, olive skin?"

"Green eyes, but the rest is true."

"Send him. Seven o'clock. Wait, make it six. I want him here before anyone else."

In other words, she wanted to fuck him before the party started. The thought of Andre having sex with another woman made Michelle's stomach clench. "I'll give him directions to your place. Shall I use the same credit card number I have on file?"

"Yes, that one is fine. If he's as hunky as you say, I'll give him a bonus."

I'll bet. "Coopers' Companions wants you to be satisfied, Ms. Dubois."

"With a gorgeous Italian, I'm sure I will be. Ta-ta."

Slowly, Michelle replaced the receiver in its cradle. A thousand butterflies played dive bomber in her stomach. She had to call Andre and tell him he had a date in a few hours. She didn't want to. She didn't want him anywhere near Angela Dubois.

"Hey, sis."

Michelle had been so wrapped up with thoughts of Andre and Angela that she hadn't heard the front door open. She looked up to see Brent slide into the chair next to her desk. "Hey, bro."

He frowned. "What's wrong?"

"Nothing."

"C'mon, Chelle, I know you. What is it?"

Michelle easily confided in Zach. Confiding in Brent wasn't as easy. He got angry much too quickly. "Angela Dubois just called. She wanted an escort for a party at her place tonight."

"And this is a problem…why?"

"She didn't want Peter or Reese. The only escort I had left was Andre."

"I still don't see the problem."

"She's a barracuda! She'll bite Andre and spit him out."

Brent's eyes twinkled with laughter. He slouched down in his chair and crossed his ankles. "Maybe Andre will enjoy getting bitten."

Michelle scowled at her brother. "You aren't helping."

"Well, hell, Michelle, I honestly don't see the problem."

"You know Angela Dubois always wants sex with her escort."

"Yeah, I know that. She pays a good price for it too." He hooked his fingers together over his stomach. "Our escorts sign on knowing all the rules. We don't push sex with the clients. That isn't who we are. But the guys know sex is a possibility every time they escort a woman. Andre is no different. He knew the rules before he took out the first woman." He cocked his head. "Or maybe he *is* different. What's going on between you and him?"

"Nothing. We had dinner together last night. That's all."

"If it was only dinner, how come you have a hickey on your neck?"

Michelle quickly covered the dark mark with her hand as heat flooded her face. She hadn't expected to see Brent today, so had pulled her hair back in a ponytail instead of leaving it down.

"He worked fast." Brent's eyes narrowed. "I don't like that."

His over-protective attitude was exactly why Michelle didn't like to confide in Brent. "Didn't we already have this conversation? It takes two to make love, Brent. Andre did nothing wrong."

"You don't even *know* him."

"I know him a lot better after last night."

"Shit!" Brent surged to his feet and took three steps away from the desk before facing her again. "You don't have sex with a stranger, Michelle."

"Andre isn't a stranger. Besides, you have sex with women you don't know."

"That's completely different."

"What a convenient argument."

"Arrgh!" Brent pushed one hand through his hair. "Why are you so goddamn hard-headed?"

"Why are you such a chauvinist?"

"A...what?"

"You heard me." Michelle stood, emphasizing her words by poking her forefinger into his chest. "You still think there are two sets of rules for men and women. Well, there aren't. If I want to have sex with a different man every night, I have the right to do that."

"You're my *sister*, Michelle."

"I'm a woman too, Brent. You have a hard time remembering that."

He stared at her for several moments before releasing a heavy sigh. "Yeah," he said softly, "I do have a hard time remembering that."

His admission surprised her. "Excuse me?"

"I still think of you as my little sister. Not *younger*, but *little*." He touched the tip of her nose. "These freckles don't help you look any older."

"Thanks," she said dryly.

He slid his hands into the front pockets of his jeans. "I guess I take the protective big-brother role too seriously."

"You think?"

Brent scowled at her. "You could help make this apology a bit easier."

"No, I can't." She grinned. "I like it when you grovel."

"Excuse me," Andre said from the doorway.

Michelle's heartbeat kicked into overdrive at the sound of Andre's voice. She whirled around and smiled at him. "Hi."

"I do not wish to interrupt a private conversation—"

"You aren't. We were just chatting."

Andre looked at Brent. "May I speak with Michelle alone?"

Brent glanced from Andre to Michelle and back again. "Sure. No problem."

Once Brent had left the room, closing the door behind him, Andre stepped closer to her. Michelle held her breath as he lifted her chin with one forefinger and dropped a soft kiss on her lips. "Hello."

She smiled again. "Hello."

"I know you have to work, but I could not wait any longer to see you."

Standing next to Andre, looking into his emerald green eyes, made her knees weak. "I can take a break."

"I am hoping for more than that. Have dinner with me tonight."

The warm, fuzzy feeling in her stomach dropped to her feet. "I can't."

He cradled her neck in his palm. "You have other plans?"

"No. *You* do."

"Pardon?"

Michelle moved to her desk and picked up the piece of paper where she'd jotted down Angela Dubois' address. "I've arranged an escort job for you tonight."

She nibbled on her bottom lip as Andre took the paper from her. "She's a regular client. I offered to send Peter or Reese, but she said she'd already dated them and wanted someone new. You were the only escort available."

"It is fine." He folded the paper and slipped it into the back pocket of his jeans. "It is my job, is it not?"

"Yes, but…"

He tilted his head. "But?"

Michelle blew out a breath. "Angela is very seductive. She always wants sex from my escorts."

"And you are worried the same will happen with me?"

Looking away from him, she swallowed hard. She had no right to ask anything of Andre after only one night together. Still…

"Michelle." He cupped her cheek and turned her face back toward his. He smiled tenderly. "When you interviewed Nathan and me, you told us it is up to the escort if he wants a more intimate ending to a date, that your client would not be upset should he resist her advances. Is that not true?"

She nodded.

"I have no desire for another woman. I only want you."

"You haven't seen Angela Dubois. She's gorgeous."

"She cannot be any more gorgeous than you."

His sweet words warmed her heart. "Thank you."

"I am being honest." He ran his thumb over her lips. "I do not think you realize how attractive you are."

"You must have a thing for freckles."

"I do." His gaze passed over her face. "I would like to kiss you for every freckle you have."

Michelle sighed to herself. This man knew exactly what to say to make a woman melt. "That's a lot of kisses."

"I like kissing."

"Me too," she whispered.

He covered her lips with his. Angling his head, he parted her lips with his tongue and deepened the kiss. Michelle tunneled her fingers into his thick hair and returned his kiss. It grew hotter, wetter, more intense, until she was fighting for breath.

She went willingly when he backed her up to the wall and stepped between her legs. He pumped his hips, brushing her clit with his hard cock.

It wouldn't take much more of that to make her come without even taking off her clothes.

"Your brother," Andre whispered against her lips.

"Won't bother us."

He filled his hands with her breasts as he kissed her again. "You are sure?"

Michelle moaned when he plucked at her nipples. "I'm sure."

Quickly he pulled her jeans and panties down her legs. Michelle unfastened the snap and zipper on Andre's jeans, releasing that glorious cock. Sliding his arms beneath her knees, he lifted and spread her legs wide. He slid into her pussy with one long thrust.

Michelle gripped his head and closed her eyes, absorbing the feel of his shaft filling her so completely. There was no easy build-up like last night. Andre fucked her hard and fast, the sound of flesh slapping against flesh filling the room. Each thrust of his hard staff into her pussy brushed her clit. Her breathing hitched as her desire climbed higher.

He fastened his mouth on her neck and sucked hard. Michelle felt that sucking all the way in her womb.

"You're giving me another hickey."

"Mmmmm," Andre mumbled, his mouth still pressed to her neck.

"Do you want the whole world to see it?"

He released her neck and nipped her earlobe. "I want the whole world to know I'm fucking you."

His graphic words together with his pounding cock pushed her over the peak. The orgasm slithered through her body from her head to her toes. Pressing her lips together to keep from crying out, she threw back her head and rode the waves. She'd barely come down from the heavens when she felt Andre tense. Moaning loudly, he buried his face between her neck and shoulder. He pumped again and again, then remained still.

Andre lifted his head and looked into her eyes. A teasing light turned his green eyes emerald. "Fucking is such a wonderful invention. It must be Italian."

Michelle burst out laughing.

"Shh." He grinned before kissing her. "Your brother will hear you."

"If he didn't hear you pounding me against the wall, he won't hear me laughing."

"You do not like being pounded against the wall?"

"I *love* it."

"And you came."

"I most certainly did."

"So you can come if you're on top of a man, and if he pounds you against the wall."

She didn't understand how she could feel like laughing when the aftershocks of her orgasm still gripped her. "It takes a special man to make me come by pounding me against a wall."

"Ah." He grinned wickedly. "So I am a special man?"

"Yes. You're very special."

All traces of amusement faded from his expression. "So are you."

He kissed her softly, sweetly, before letting her feet slide back to the floor. Warm wetness trickled from her channel when he pulled his shaft from her body, a combination of her juices and his. "I, uh, need to clean up."

Andre nodded toward the open door. "Is that not a bathroom?"

"Yes."

"If you will hand me a washcloth, I will leave you to your privacy."

She showed him her appreciation for his thoughtfulness with a kiss. "Thank you."

* * * * *

Five minutes later, she walked him to the front door, their fingers clasped together. She didn't want to let him go. It had been much too long since she'd experienced such a strong attraction to a man. She longed to savor this feeling of burgeoning...

Michelle didn't know if she could call it love, not this soon. She and Andre barely knew each other. It must take more than one date to fall in love.

Well, one date and one wall pounding.

His cell phone beeped as they reached the door. Andre removed it from the clip on his belt and flipped it open. He smiled.

"A text message from Nathan. He is leaving Houston now. He finished his assignment early."

"His assignment?"

"He took pictures of the new art museum for some magazine. He told me the name, but I cannot remember it now. He hopes it will help him get a showing of his own."

"A showing? He's that good?"

"Nathan is an excellent photographer. Ask him to show you his work."

"Will he? You won't let me read your book."

"I did not say no. I said I would think about it."

"So will you let me read it?"

He grinned. "Maybe."

Before she could sputter a complaint, he kissed her quickly. "I will talk to you later."

Michelle leaned against the door, sighing happily. What an incredible man. Handsome, charming, funny, sexy.

Her heart had stumbled when Andre mentioned Nathan, but that meant nothing. Not anymore. She couldn't imagine any other man making her feel as wonderful as she did right now.

Chapter Eight

8>

Nathan walked into the apartment and dropped his suitcase. The long drive from Houston had zapped his strength. He knew he should unpack, but had no desire to do it now. He wanted a drink first, then just to collapse on the couch in front of the TV and not move for the rest of the night.

Of course, if Andre wanted to fuck, Nathan was sure his strength would quickly return. A hard cock up his ass would revive him better than a hot shower.

"Andre?"

"In here."

He made his way to the kitchen. He found Andre at the table, pecking on his notebook keys. "Hey."

"Hey." Andre looked up and smiled. "How'd it go?"

"Good. The museum is incredible. You could spend a whole day in it with no problem."

"I'll go with you next time."

"Deal." Nathan walked over to the refrigerator, stopping at Andre's side long enough to kiss him. "You want a beer?"

"No, I'm sticking with iced tea. I have a date tonight."

Returning to the table, Nathan slouched in his chair and opened his beer. "Another date with Michelle so soon?"

"No, this is an escort date." Andre pressed a few keys and shut the notebook. "I wish it were Michelle instead."

Nathan took a long drink of the cold brew. "So, how was it?"

Andre smiled wickedly. "Delicious."

Nathan groaned. "Shit, I'm jealous."

"She is… A single adjective isn't strong enough to describe her. Absolutely charming. Graceful. Perfect manners at the restaurant. A bit shy at first, but that shyness disappeared in the bedroom. She is *hot* in bed."

"Is her body as gorgeous as I've imagined it?"

"Probably more than you've imagined. Her breasts are incredible and she has nice big nipples. There's a little tuft of hair on her mound. Other than that, she shaves her pussy."

Nathan's cock began to react at the thought of pushing his tongue all the way inside her. "Taste good?"

Andre kissed the tips of his fingers in a classic Italian gesture. "*Delizioso.*"

Pushing aside his notebook, Andre leaned forward and rested his forearms on the table. "I went to see her this morning. I fucked her against the wall in her office. Brent was somewhere in the house."

Nathan shook his head at Andre's nerve. "You've got balls, man."

"She said he wouldn't interrupt us and he didn't. God, she has a sweet pussy." He groaned softly. "Damn. Thinking about it is giving me a hard-on."

Nathan liked the sound of that. His own growing hard-on could use some attention. "Want some help with that boner?"

"I'd love to stick it down your throat, but I want you to find Michelle instead and take her out tonight."

"Just like that? She might say no."

"I believe she's attracted to you. Yeah, our sex was great, but when I told her about your photography this morning, her eyes sparkled with interest."

"For my photography, or for me?"

"I think it's both. She wants to look at your work. You should go by the office. She told me she'd be there until six. She said she gets a lot of calls on Friday for dates on Saturday, and she had more paperwork to do."

Nathan rubbed his chin. "I could print out a few pictures and take them to her, maybe ask her out to dinner."

"I think that's an excellent idea. No, wait. I have a better idea. Don't take anything to her. Bring her back here to show her your work. I'll be home late, so I won't be in your way."

"Maybe I want you in the way. It would be a perfect opportunity for the three of us to be together."

Picking up his glass of tea, Andre leaned back in his chair. "I think you should be with her first by yourself. Get a taste of that heat."

Nathan shifted in his chair. "Shit man, I'm already hard."

Andre grinned. "Go see her."

"You've talked me into it." He took a final gulp of his beer and set the bottle on the table. "I'm gonna grab a shower first."

"Go ahead. I'll write a bit more before I get ready for my date."

Nathan stopped in the doorway and looked back at Andre. "Do you know anything about your date?"

"It's a party at her penthouse. Michelle said she's filthy rich and gorgeous. That's all I know."

"What if she wants more than your escort services?"

"Michelle told me this Angela always wants sex with her escorts. She'll be disappointed this time. Michelle is the only woman I want to be with."

"So you're really sure she's the one?"

"You'll be sure too, the first time you kiss her."

"Sounds good."

"Oh, and one other thing. She said it's easier for her to come on top."

Nathan grinned. "No problem there."

* * * * *

Michelle stuck out her tongue at her computer. "Stupid machine. Why do you give me so much trouble?"

"To drive you crazy."

The sound of Nathan's voice surprised her. She hadn't heard him come in the front door. This was the second time today someone had come in and she hadn't heard the bell tinkle. She made a mental note to have Brent check it. "Nathan. Hi."

"Hi." Smiling, he sat in the chair by her desk. "Am I interrupting?"

"No. I was about to throw my computer out the window. You saved her life."

Nathan chuckled. "Your computer is a she?"

"Cleo. I always name my computers. This one..." she glared at the monitor, "has tried my patience ever since I bought her two months ago."

"Maybe you should take it back where you bought it. Excuse me. Maybe you should take *her* back."

"I refuse to give up."

"Good for you." He rose and moved to stand behind her chair. "Let me help. I'm pretty good with computers. I fix Andre's when he has a problem."

"You didn't come over here to help me. What can I do for you?"

"We'll get to me in a minute." He leaned down until their faces were only a few inches apart. "I'd like to help."

Such gorgeous chocolate brown eyes, surrounded by thick eyelashes. His face was close enough to hers so that she saw her reflection in the dark depths. He smelled good too...clean, fresh, as if he'd showered recently. His cheeks were smooth, but stubble covered his upper lip. Without considering the intimacy of her move, she reached out and touched the stubble with one fingertip. "You missed shaving here."

A crooked grin tilted up one corner of his mouth. "I'm growing a mustache. I've thought about it for a while and decided, what the hell."

She suspected it'd be thick and full, a bit darker than the hair on his head. Michelle had never been a fan of beards, but she loved mustaches. She especially loved kissing a man who had a mustache.

Nathan licked his bottom lip. His lips parted as he leaned closer to her...

What are you doing?

Jerking herself out of the sensual trance, she turned back toward her computer. "I'm getting ready to leave. Let's not worry about this now, okay?"

"Sure."

He returned to his chair, propping one ankle on the opposite knee. The position emphasized the nice bulge at his crotch.

What is wrong *with you? You made love with Andre a few hours ago in this room! You can't have any feelings for Nathan.*

But she did. She wanted to be with him as much as she wanted to be with Andre.

"Andre has a date tonight," Nathan said, lacing his fingers over his stomach. "I don't feel like eating alone. Have dinner with me."

Michelle quickly shook her head. "I can't."

"You have plans?"

"Paperwork. Lots of paperwork."

"You just said you're getting ready to leave."

He had her there. Michelle sighed. The best thing now would be honesty.

"Nathan, did you talk to Andre before you came here?"

"Briefly. He was pecking on his notebook when I got home. I said a fast hi and bye before I hit the shower. Why?"

"Did he tell you we went out last night?"

Nathan nodded. "You went to an Italian restaurant. He said the food was great."

"It was." She picked up a pen from the desk and laid it right back down again. "Did he tell you anything…else?"

He tilted his head. "Like?"

"Well, like…" She stopped, unsure how to ask if Andre had told his roommate about their lovemaking.

Nathan smiled tenderly. "Michelle, if you're trying to ask me if I know you and Andre made love, yeah, I know. It's pretty obvious by the hickeys."

I gotta remember to wear my hair down. Michelle clenched her hands together to keep from covering the marks on her neck.

"You think I'm assuming I'll score with you just because you were with Andre? It doesn't work that way, Michelle. Andre and I don't share our women." That crooked grin touched his lips again. "Unless they want us to."

Heat scurried through her body. Oh, the mental picture that popped into her head of these two men playing with her…

Nathan leaned forward in his chair. "I want to try some genuine Texas barbecue. How about it? Be my tour guide tonight. No strings, no expectations. Just two friends eating together."

Michelle believed him. They could go out, have a good time. That didn't mean she'd take him home with her.

No matter how strong the attraction she felt for him.

"You want real Texas barbecue? You got it."

* * * * *

Nathan leaned forward so Michelle could hear him over Willie Nelson's twang. "You know what?"

She leaned forward also, resting her forearms on the table. "What?"

"You look cute in my hat."

Grinning, she rolled her bottle of beer between her palms. "You plunked it on my head. Possession is nine-tenths of the law. Or something like that."

Nathan chuckled. She really was cute. Her hair tumbled over her shoulders in soft curls. The straw cowboy hat sat atop those curls. She'd told him he'd never fit in as a Texan until he had a straw cowboy hat and a pair of leather boots. He went along with her when she dragged him into a Western clothing store. He passed on the boots, but agreed to buy the hat. Deciding it would look better on her, he'd placed it on her head once they left the store. She'd worn it for the last hour.

She completely enchanted him.

"Plunked. I like that."

"You've never used that word?"

"Not that I can remember, no."

"You've probably never used yonder or y'all either."

"Uh, no. What's a yonder?"

"Your education has been sadly lacking, Nathan." She took a sip of her beer. "Yonder is a place. You know, like when you're giving directions. You say, 'he lives over yonder.'"

"And how far away is yonder?"

"However far you need it to be."

"There's absolutely no logic in that."

"There doesn't have to be. This is Texas."

Nathan laughed. Her charming accent became even stronger when she talked about her state. "I've missed so much in my life."

"Well, you're here now. You can make up for lost time."

He'd like to start with her. Nathan watched her as he sipped his own beer. Since he was driving, he'd limited himself to one drink. Besides, he wanted to be clear-headed so he could enjoy every moment with Michelle.

"Would you like to dance?"

Michelle scrunched up her nose. "Honestly? I'd rather take a walk. I'm not a country music fan."

"So why are we here?"

"'Cause it has the best barbecue in the city."

"We've eaten. Let's go for a walk."

After taking care of the check, Nathan slipped his arm around Michelle's waist to lead her through the crowd. Once outside, he laced their fingers together as they strolled down the sidewalk. She didn't complain. He took that as a sign that she was enjoying their time together.

They walked silently, Nathan nodding to the people who passed them. Words weren't necessary. He was content to simply be with Michelle.

"Autumn begins tomorrow," Michelle said, breaking the silence. "I'm *so* ready for it."

"Tired of summer?"

"Oh, yeah. I like the sun and the warm weather, but it gets old after six months. I'm ready to curl up on my couch with an afghan over my legs and a cup of hot chocolate."

"Sounds good." He tugged her closer to him so a couple could pass them on the sidewalk. "So is autumn your favorite season?"

"Yes. I wish we had more trees in the area that changed color. We have some, but nothing like what's in other parts of the country."

She'd given him the perfect opportunity to talk about his photography. "You'd love the trees in the Midwest. I'd go out every weekend in the fall and take pictures of the trees. Incredible."

"Andre told me you're an excellent photographer."

Nathan shrugged. "I don't know about that, but I enjoy it."

Michelle stopped walking. "Can I see some of your pictures?"

"Sure. I'd be happy to share my work with you."

"When?"

"Now is good for me."

She smiled. "I'd like that."

He had to take her to his apartment to show her the photographs. Once he got her there, he had every intention of making love with her. He wouldn't push. Nathan had never pushed anyone for sex in his life. But the way she smiled at him, the way her eyes clearly showed desire when she looked at him, told him he wouldn't have to push.

She'd be his…soon.

Chapter Nine

&

From what Andre had said about his and Nathan's housekeeping abilities, Michelle expected to see piles of newspapers on the floor, dirty dishes on every flat surface, and dust on the furniture. Instead, the living room was neat and tidy, no evidence of newspapers or dirty dishes anywhere.

"Nice."

"Andre would be glad to hear you say that. He spent all afternoon straightening up the place."

"He told me you're neater than he is."

"Housework isn't on my list of fun things to do." He motioned toward the couch. "Have a seat. Do you want something to drink? I think Andre has some white wine in the fridge."

"Wine would be nice."

He smiled. "Be right back."

Michelle perched on the edge of the couch. She wanted to see Nathan's work, but wondered if it had been a mistake for her to come here. She'd been intimate with Andre last night and earlier today. Although she and Andre weren't involved in a serious relationship, it seemed like she was cheating to be on a date with Nathan.

She liked him. He made her laugh. Her sides actually began to hurt from laughing so much while they were shopping for his hat. He had a quick wit, a devilish smile, killer eyes.

Andre was old-world charming and romantic. Nathan was fun and easygoing. They both made her heart beat funny.

She watched Nathan come back into the room. He carried two wine glasses in one hand, a bottle of wine in the other. A thick brown album was nestled beneath his arm.

"Living with a guy who grew up in a vineyard means we always have wine." He sat next to her, placing the bottle and glasses on the coffee table. "I like it, but I don't know one brand from another. Andre can spout dates and brands and types as if he has a little computer in his brain." He slipped the album onto the table too, then poured her wine. "Me, I'm a beer guy most of the time."

Michelle accepted the glass from him, holding it between her palms while he poured his own glass. "Beer goes with barbecue."

"And hot dogs and chicken wings and grilled hamburgers."

"You're a junk food addict."

"Guilty as charged. It's a good thing Andre does most of the cooking. He tries to keep me healthy."

She let her gaze travel over his toned body. She couldn't see where his love of junk food showed. "You must work out."

"I have to or Andre would kick me out." He held out his glass to her. "To friends, both old and new."

"To friends." She clinked her glass against his and sipped her wine. It was dry and crisp and warmed her as it slid down her throat.

"How about some music?" Nathan asked, picking up a remote control from the coffee table. "What's your preference?"

"I like classic rock from the sixties and seventies, but I'll listen to whatever you want to."

He pointed the remote toward the stereo in the entertainment center along the wall. The Eagles' "Desperado" filled the air. Michelle smiled. "You like classic rock too?"

"Yep. Andre prefers classical. I'll listen to it, but give me the Eagles or Stones any day."

Michelle took another sip of her wine before gesturing toward the album. "Is that your portfolio?"

"I don't know if I'd call it a portfolio. These are some of my favorite shots."

"Do you use a digital or film camera?"

"Both. Most of these were taken with film. They're all eight-by-tens."

Setting her glass on the table, she reached for the album. Nathan leaned back against the couch, one arm across the back. She nestled against his side and opened the album.

The first one took her breath. "Oh my."

"I took that two years ago when we went to Italy to visit his family."

Andre stood among the grapevines. He held a bunch of red grapes in his hand, looking down at them as if examining their quality. The sky was overcast with thick roiling clouds. It must have been windy, for Andre's hair was tousled.

Nathan had given it the caption, *Master of the Grapes.*

"It's wonderful."

"Andre is a perfect model."

There were several pictures of Andre mixed in with colorful scenery shots—working on his computer, lounging in a chair, reading a book. A black-and-white photo of him dressed in jeans and an unbuttoned shirt made her mouth water.

Michelle started to turn another page, but Nathan touched her hand before she could. "I took the next one last week."

Curious, she turned the page...and gasped. She saw herself surrounded by flowers in the backyard of Coopers' Companions. She was on her knees, her hands on her thighs.

Her head was tilted back, her eyes closed. The sun bathed her face. A tiny smile touched her lips. She looked…

Beautiful.

"I watched you for a few minutes while you were working in the flowers. You seemed to be really enjoying what you were doing. When you stopped and tilted your head back like that, I couldn't resist taking the shot."

All of Nathan's photographs were in sheet protectors. Still, she gently touched the photo of herself, not wanting to smudge it in any way. He'd labeled it *Michelle Among the Flowers*. "I don't know what to say."

"I have other pictures of you, but this is my favorite."

She looked up into his face. "You've taken pictures of me?"

He nodded. "I know I should've told you. Are you angry at me for taking pictures without telling you?"

"No, of course not. I'm…surprised. And flattered."

"Why? You have to know how I feel about you."

She had no idea what to say to that statement.

Nathan leaned closer and ran his thumb over her cheek, her jaw. "I started falling in love with you the first moment I saw you."

Michelle's heart thudded in her chest and her stomach did a flip-flop. This incredible man, a man who could easily be the model for a woman's dream guy, had just said he was falling in love with her. So many thoughts flashed through her mind, she couldn't put them together well enough to make a coherent sentence.

She didn't have to speak. Nathan's kiss said everything.

Cradling her jaw, he tilted her head back and covered her lips with his. His hat tumbled from her head and fell to the floor. Michelle didn't care. She drank in the taste of Nathan—the crisp bite of wine on his tongue, the faint hint of barbecue, the unique flavor of *him*.

The combination was intoxicating.

He leaned closer to her, until his chest touched her breasts. Michelle's nipples puckered at the contact. She moaned softly and pressed her breasts against him. It wasn't enough. She needed more of him, more of the two of them together.

She went willingly when he coaxed her down to the couch.

"Michelle," Nathan whispered, his breath coasting over her lips.

His tongue circled her lips, seeking entrance. She gave it, brushing her tongue over his. He groaned deep in his throat and deepened the kiss. His tongue stroked, darted, as he pumped his hips. With each movement, he pushed his hard cock farther between her legs.

"I want you." He kissed her cheek, her jaw, the dark marks that Andre had left on her neck. Tugging on the neckline of her T-shirt, he nipped the soft swell of her breast. "I want you naked beneath me."

"Nathan," she rasped.

She arched her neck and lifted her hips, rubbing her pussy against his shaft. It'd been a long time since Nathan had been so turned on that he was in danger of coming in his jeans. He had to slow things down before he did exactly that.

"Tell me you want me. If you don't, this stops right now."

She touched his face, her fingertips gliding over his skin. "I want you."

"Are you sure? I don't want to come between you and Andre."

"I'm sure," she said before kissing him again.

He rose to his knees between her thighs. Taking the hem of her shirt, he tugged it over her head and tossed it to the floor. She wore a pale blue, lacy bra with the hook in the front. Looking into her eyes, he unfastened the hook and drew the cups back from her breasts. Once her breasts were bare, he looked at them.

"Jesus," he whispered. He filled his hands with her firm flesh, gliding his thumbs over the rosy nipples. He wished he knew some of Andre's fancy Italian words. Such perfection deserved to be praised with beautiful words. "These are incredible." Leaning forward, he licked one hard nub, then the other. "Do they need to be sucked?"

"Oh, yes."

"You like that?"

She tunneled her fingers into his hair, holding his head close to her. "Don't talk. Suck."

Nathan parted his lips over the tip of her breast. He liked when a woman wasn't afraid to tell her lover what she wanted. Wanting to please her, he drew her nipple into his mouth, suckling deeply.

"Don't stop," Michelle moaned.

He had no desire to stop. He sucked harder as he slipped his hand between their bodies. A flick of his thumb unbuttoned her jeans. The gentle rasp of the zipper sounded loud in the still room. He slid his hand inside her panties. Warm, wet cream covered his fingers.

His cock jerked inside his jeans.

"Rub my clit."

Releasing her nipple, he kissed her again. "I have a better idea."

"What?"

"How about if I lick it instead?"

Her lids lowered, her lips fell open. "Yesssss."

Moments later, she lay naked before him. Nathan ran his hands up her legs, over her stomach, her breasts. Andre was right. Her body was even more exquisite than he'd imagined. He kissed her once more, pressing his tongue deep into her mouth. Dropping to his knees, he draped her legs over his shoulders. He gave her pussy a long lick from anus to clit.

"Oh, I love that." She threw her arms over her head and lifted her hips. "More."

"Where do you want my tongue? Here?" He parted her feminine lips with his thumbs and licked the moist opening to her body. "Here?" The tip of his tongue tickled her clit. "Or here?" He drove his tongue into her ass.

"Everywhere. All of it."

If she wanted it all, he'd give it to her, for as long as she needed it. Pulling her labia farther apart, he licked, sucked, worshipped her wet flesh. The more he lapped up her juices, the more her body created.

She tasted better than the finest wine, the richest chocolate.

Her breathing grew heavier, quicker. Nathan suckled her clit as he pushed his thumb into her ass. She trembled, moaned, before collapsing back on the couch.

Leaning back on his heels, Nathan wiped her juices from his chin. God, she was a passionate woman. He could hardly wait to sink his cock into her heat.

Michelle slowly opened her eyes. Nathan was on his knees on the floor, still fully clothed. Two nights in a row she'd been naked while her lover still wore clothes. There was something decadent about that.

Propping up on one elbow, she laid her hand over the large bulge behind his zipper. "Want some help with this?"

She watched him stand and pull his shirt over his head. He toed off his shoes while unfastening his jeans. She gasped when he pushed his jeans past his hips. He didn't wear underwear either. She only had a moment to admire his glorious thick cock before he tugged her to her feet. He sat down on the couch and pulled her to his lap, her legs straddling his.

"Ride me," he rasped.

She grasped his shaft and lowered herself over it. He clutched her hips as she began to move.

"That's the way. Ride my cock. Take it all."

An orgasm should've left her satisfied. It didn't. Michelle wanted more…wanted to feel that breath-stealing pleasure rush through her body again. She moved faster, the sound of his flesh sliding into hers mixing with their heavy breathing. She wrapped her arms around his neck. She kissed his lips, his jaw, his neck, savoring his scent and taste. The pleasure built inside her body again, even more powerful than a few minutes ago.

"Come for me, Michelle. I want to feel your pussy grab my cock when you come."

Throwing back her head, she bit her bottom lip and keened as the orgasm rushed through her body. Nathan crushed her to him, his body trembling from his own release.

Moments passed while he held her. Michelle sighed softly, totally content to be in Nathan's arms.

A soft kiss fell on her neck. She raised her head and looked into his eyes. He smiled. "Hi."

Michelle smiled back. "Hi."

"I wouldn't mind doing that again in a few minutes."

"Only a few minutes?"

"Mmm-hmm." He caressed her breasts, lifting and squeezing them. "I recuperate fast."

"Every woman's dream."

Nathan gently twisted her nipples. She hitched in a breath at the sharp sensation. It hurt and felt good at the same time.

"I love your nipples. Nice and big and hard." He twisted them again, and Michelle moaned. "You like this, don't you?"

"It feels good."

"Have you ever worn nipple clamps?"

She shook her head.

"Would you let me do that to you?"

The thought of it sent a zing through her clit. She'd never participated in any kind of bondage, but she'd thought about it…fantasized about it. She nodded.

"*Jesus*, babe."

He arched his hips. Michelle's eyes widened at the feel of his shaft growing firm again inside her. "You do recuperate fast."

"Yeah," he croaked. "Put your arms around my neck and hold on."

The next moment, Michelle found herself on her back on the soft carpet with Nathan holding her arms over her head. He began to move his hips, thrusting his cock into her pussy.

"You are so hot." He kissed her lips, then buried his face against her neck as he continued to pump his hips. "My God, I love fucking you."

He still held her arms so she couldn't touch him with her hands, but she wrapped her legs around his thighs. His skin grew slick with sweat. His heart thumped against her breast as his damp body slid over hers. She had no doubt he was about to have another climax.

He surprised her by rolling them over so he was on his back with her on top.

"I'm too close to coming," he said, pushing her to a sitting position. "You're in charge now."

Michelle liked being in charge. Bracing her hands on Nathan's chest, she clenched her internal muscles and squeezed his shaft. He groaned.

"That won't stop me from coming."

"I'm not trying to stop you."

Sliding his thumb between her legs, he massaged her clit. "Come with me."

He found all the sensitive nerve endings and brought them back to life. Michelle began to ride him again, taking him as deep inside her as she could. Nathan continued the attention to her clit with one hand while rubbing her breasts with the other.

A sharp tug on her nipple, and the orgasm flooded her body.

Michelle collapsed on Nathan's chest, her lungs battling for air. She didn't have three orgasms during sex. She usually had one, sometimes two, but never more than that, and never so quickly. She'd swear she could feel her bones dissolving.

First Andre and now Nathan had made her body react in a way that no man had ever accomplished.

Growling deep in his throat, Nathan clasped her buttocks and arched his hips. She dropped soft kisses on his chest as he relaxed and lay still again. He ran his hands up and down her spine in a gentle caress. Totally satisfied, her eyes drifted closed.

"I didn't wear a condom."

Michelle propped her chin on her hands and looked at him. "I know you're clean. So am I. And before you ask the next question, I'm on the Pill."

"Not a very romantic subject, huh?"

"But a necessary one."

He ran his fingers through her hair. "Stay with me tonight," he whispered.

She'd love to. Waking up in Nathan's arms tomorrow morning would be wonderful. But she couldn't. She didn't know how she'd face Andre after being intimate with Nathan. "I think it'd be better if I went home."

He remained silent for several moments, his hands traveling up and down her spine and over her buttocks. "Any chance I could change your mind?" He grinned crookedly. "I'd lick your pussy again."

Michelle chuckled, but quickly grew serious again. "No," she said softly.

He cradled her face in his hands and tugged her closer for a long kiss. "Then I'll take you home."

Chapter Ten

ഔ

Michelle laid her spoon on the table and sighed heavily. "I am a total slut."

Breanna looked at her over the rim of her mug as she sipped her latte. "Why do you say that?"

"Because I had sex with Andre and Nathan."

"At the same time?"

"No! But on the same day."

"When?"

"Yesterday."

"Oh yeah?" Setting down her mug, Breanna leaned forward, her eyes wide. "Give me *all* the details. And don't leave out *anything*. You owe me for waking me up so early."

Michelle had called Breanna first thing this morning. She'd told her sleepy and grumpy friend that she desperately needed to talk. The anxiety in her voice must have finally seeped into Bre's brain. It had taken her less than half an hour to meet Michelle at their favorite coffee shop.

Propping her elbow on the table, Michelle covered her eyes with her hand. "I can't believe I did that."

"Stop putting yourself down. You didn't do anything wrong."

She looked back at her friend. "You don't think having sex with two different men the same day is *wrong*?"

"No, I don't." She grinned. "It makes you sexually adventurous."

Michelle groaned. Naturally Breanna would think having sex with both Andre and Nathan was peachy. She loved sex as often as possible.

Breanna picked up her mug and held it in both hands. "Tell me what happened."

"I had dinner with Andre Thursday night. He took me to Paul's Garden."

"Paul's Garden? Wow. Is it as incredible as I've heard?"

She nodded. "The food was delicious, the décor beautiful. Andre was the perfect date. Charming, attentive, polite. He's just...perfect."

"In bed too?"

"Oh, yes. He was a bit dominant. That was an incredible turn-on."

"A strong man in the bedroom is a definite turn-on."

"He spent the night with me. Then the next day, he came to see me at the office. He fucked me against the wall."

Breanna moaned. "Ohmigod, that's hot."

Michelle grinned at the glassy look in her friend's eyes. "It certainly was." Her grin faded. "So explain to me why I agreed to go out with Nathan only a few hours later."

"Because Nathan is just as hot as Andre."

"That's for sure." Michelle glanced around their area to be sure no one could hear her. "They both have amazing tongues."

"Stop it! You're hurting me. I haven't had sex in over a month. I'm even considering dipping into my trust fund and hiring one of your escorts."

"You could go out with Brent."

"Puh-*leese*! I'm not *that* desperate."

"And what's wrong with my brother? He's a hunk."

"I didn't say he isn't a hunk. Brent is gorgeous. He's just not my type." She wiggled her mouth back and forth. "Although he does have a nice bulge behind his fly."

Michelle pushed her hair behind her ears. "I didn't need to hear that."

Breanna grinned. "You brought him into the conversation." She took another sip of her latte. "Back to you. Are they good kissers?"

"The best."

"Which one is the better lover?"

"I couldn't possibly choose. I came so many times, I almost passed out. That's *never* happened to me. They're incredible. Different techniques, different movements, but they both dissolved my bones."

"Dissolving bones is good." She set her mug on the table and leaned back in her chair. "The answer to all this is simple, Chelle. You're attracted to both of them."

"I *can't* be! I can't be involved with two men."

"I don't see why not. Go for it. Keep seeing Andre and Nathan and decide which one you care about the most."

Drumming her fingertips on the table, Michelle drew her bottom lip between her teeth. "Nathan told me he's falling in love with me."

Breanna's eyes widened again. "You didn't tell me that part."

"I think I'm falling in love with him too."

"There, you see? You just made your choice."

"But I feel just as strongly about Andre. I don't know how to choose between them."

"You don't have to choose, I told you that. You are in complete control, Michelle. Don't forget that."

Complete control. Yeah, right. She turned into a mush ball whenever she was near either of those edible men. "You really don't think it's bad for me to go out with both of them, at least for a while?"

"Actually, I think you should have them at the same time. Fucking two men at once is unforgettable."

A mental picture popped into Michelle's head of Andre and Nathan in bed with her. The sexy image made her clit throb. Michelle squirmed on her chair. "I thought about that. I think Andre and Nathan have shared women in the past. Nathan said something about it, that he and Andre don't share unless the woman wants them to."

"My God. Both of those hunks at once? How delicious would that be?"

Michelle couldn't imagine. Well, she *could* imagine, and that had her squirming on her chair again. "I have no idea how to ask them about this."

"I don't think you'll have to. I bet they'll bring it up to you."

"You think so?"

"Just wait. I wouldn't be surprised if you're in bed with both of them within a week."

* * * * *

Michelle signed the last paycheck and placed it in an envelope. After sealing it, she wrote Andre's name on the front. She stared at his name, wondering how his date went with Angela Dubois. She knew it was none of her business, but she couldn't help wondering if he'd had sex with Angela. Although he'd told her he wouldn't, he could have changed his mind when he saw the seductive Ms. Dubois.

The ringing telephone drew her from her thoughts. Her heart jumped when she saw Andre's cell phone number on the caller I.D. She took a breath to calm her heartbeat before picking up the receiver. "Coopers' Companions, this is Michelle."

"Good morning, Michelle."

Goose bumps erupted on her arms at the sound of his voice. "Good morning."

"Am I interrupting something important?"

"No. I'm working on the paychecks."

"That is why I am calling. I have been writing and the words are flowing well for me. I do not wish to stop. Nathan is running errands this morning and said he would pick up my check. Is that acceptable?"

"Sure, as long as you approve it."

"I appreciate that. I told Nathan I did not need the check today, but he said he would be in your area and did not mind stopping." Michelle thought she heard the rustling of papers before he spoke again. "He told me he showed you some of his work."

"Yes, he did."

She waited, but Andre didn't volunteer what else Nathan had told him about Friday night's date. They were roommates. Surely Nathan had confided in Andre, especially since she and Andre had already made love.

She wanted to know, but wasn't sure how to voice the question. "Did Nathan tell you anything else about Friday?"

"I know you and he made love. Is that what you are asking?"

"Yes," she said softly.

"Nathan and I do not keep secrets from each other, Michelle. I know everything about Friday night."

"You're not upset that I was with Nathan after being with you?"

"Do you want me to be honest?"

"Completely."

"I wish I could have watched him fuck you."

Michelle moaned at the idea of Andre watching while she and Nathan made love. Her clit throbbed and moisture leaked from her pussy, dampening her panties. She'd asked for honesty and he'd certainly given her that.

"You like that idea," he said, his voice lowered to a seductive drawl. "You would like to be with both of us at the same time…kissing you, touching you, fucking you. We would take turns sliding into that sweet pussy. Or perhaps you would prefer one of us to fuck your ass. Nathan and I both enjoy that."

"Don't," she hissed.

"Am I saying something wrong?"

"No, but…I can't think when you talk like that."

"Is your clit on fire with the need to be rubbed, licked?"

"Yes."

"When you hang up the phone, will you masturbate?"

The man certainly didn't believe in mincing words. "I can't. Some of the guys will be coming in for their checks."

"But you want to, don't you? You wish you could make yourself come right now."

"Yes," she whispered.

"Do you pleasure yourself often, Michelle?"

She didn't answer him for she heard the front door open. Nathan walked into the office.

Her pussy wept again.

"Nathan is here," she told Andre.

"Let me speak to him please."

Michelle held out the receiver toward Nathan. "It's Andre."

"Thanks." Smiling, he spoke into the phone. "Hey, what's up?"

Michelle watched his face as he listened to his roommate. The smile faded from his lips. His eyes narrowed slightly.

"No problem," Nathan said. He looked back at her, and she inhaled sharply when she saw the fire in his eyes. "It'll be my pleasure."

Oh, shit. What did Andre tell him?

After replacing the receiver, he rounded the desk to where she sat. Grasping the arms of her chair, he turned her toward him and bent down so his face was close to hers. "Andre said the two of you were having an interesting conversation about masturbation."

She couldn't help it. Her gaze dipped to his crotch. She could see his cock growing, filling the area behind his fly.

Those buttons on his jeans were in danger of popping open at any moment.

The outline of his cock head was very apparent, reminding her that he didn't wear briefs. Jerking her gaze away from that tempting sight, she looked back into his eyes. "What-what else did he say?"

He laid his hands on her knees, beneath the flowery skirt she wore. He slowly pushed the skirt up her thighs as he spoke. "He said your clit needs attention. Since he isn't here, I'll be happy to help."

By now, he had her skirt bunched around her waist and was drawing her thong down her legs. "Someone could come in—"

He silenced her protest with a kiss. "I turned the deadbolt when I came in." He kissed her again as he tickled her labia with his fingertips. "Brent is the only one who can open the door."

"He-he told me he wouldn't be here until… Oh!" Her breath hitched when he strummed the sensitive nub. "Until af-after eleven."

"That gives us plenty of time." Dropping to his knees, he lifted her legs and draped them over the arms of her chair. He spread her feminine lips with his thumbs. "Mmm, you're nice and wet. I think you need a tongue. What do you think?"

Thinking wasn't even the slightest possibility now. Instead, Michelle tunneled her fingers into Nathan's short hair and drew his mouth to her pussy. "Lick me."

A long, slow swipe of tongue. Warm breath blown on wet flesh. A gentle nip of teeth. Closing her eyes, Michelle leaned her head back and concentrated on all the exquisite sensations Nathan was causing in her body. Andre's playful phone sex had already set her body on fire. Nathan's skillful tongue would quickly finish the job and drive her to orgasm.

Playtime ended. He began rapidly licking directly on her clit. He was incredible, licking and suckling her exactly the way she needed to reach the peak quickly. Releasing his head, she gripped the edge of her chair and lifted her hips closer to his mouth. "Right there. Oh, yes, right there. That's perfect. Oh. Oh. *Ohhhhhh.*"

Michelle trembled and closed her eyes as the pleasure raced through her body. She grabbed Nathan's head again, holding him still while she rode out the last wave of a powerful climax.

A soft kiss on her mouth made her sigh. The slow swipe of Nathan's tongue had her parting her lips to accept more. Her own scent drifted to her nose as he kissed her. His tongue swept inside, then across her lips before darting inside again.

Oh, my, can this man kiss!

She opened her eyes when Nathan drew away from her mouth. His jaw was clenched, his breathing heavy, his eyes hooded...all signs of arousal. Although she'd found pleasure, he hadn't.

Michelle gently pushed on his chest until he straightened. Pushing up his polo shirt to his chest, she nuzzled his flat stomach. While Andre had only a line of hair from his navel to his groin, Nathan had a nice dusting of soft blond hair on his chest and stomach. She thought it incredibly sexy.

She tickled his navel with her tongue. Nathan squeezed her shoulders while she unbuttoned his jeans. His breathing grew deeper, slower. Reaching inside his fly, Michelle drew out his hard cock. He was longer than Andre, but not as thick.

She had no complaints about the size of either one.

"Very nice," she said, caressing him with both hands. "It looks like it could use some licking too."

"Yeah," he rasped.

He tunneled his hand beneath her hair and clasped her neck. Michelle drew his cock into her mouth, an inch at a time, until her lips touched the crisp hair at the base. She breathed deeply, taking his male scent into her lungs.

Nathan's hand tightened on her neck. "God, that feels good."

The satin skin against her tongue. The musky scent of an aroused man. The intimacy and trust. Michelle loved everything about oral sex. She especially loved performing it on a man she cared about. She slid her lips back to the head before taking him deep again. He began to pump his hips, slowly fucking her mouth.

"Stick your finger up my ass."

She released his cock long enough to lick her finger, then did what he said. He rewarded her by pumping faster. "Yeah, like that. Move it in and out. Oh, yeah, that's good." He widened his stance and hunched his hips forward. "I'm gonna come, baby. All right?"

Instead of answering him with words, she pushed another finger into his ass. Nathan groaned loudly as his warmth filled her mouth.

She barely had time to lick her lips before he kissed her again. With his mouth pressed to hers, he drew her up from the chair and into his arms. Michelle wrapped her arms around his neck, tilting her head one way, then the other, while the kiss went on and on.

She did love the way he kissed.

One more soft peck and Nathan lifted his head. He smiled. "Good morning."

Tightening her arms around his neck, she raised up on tiptoes and kissed him one more time. "Good morning."

"I swear I didn't come here to seduce you."

"Then why did you lock the deadbolt?"

His hands slid down to cup her buttocks. "Well, I was hoping for a few kisses in private."

"You got those."

"And then some." He gave her a wicked grin and playfully pinched one cheek before releasing her. "I came by to get Andre's check."

"He asked me if you could. I told him no problem." She picked up Andre's envelope from the desk and handed it to him. "Now, go unlock the door in case any of my guys come for their checks."

"Sure."

It only took a few moments for Nathan to go to the door and come back to the office, but Michelle still hadn't found her thong by the time he returned. She looked under the desk, beneath the chair, against the wall. Nothing.

"What are you looking for?" he asked.

"My panties," she answered, still studying the floor. "I can't find them."

"That little scrap of fabric can't be called panties."

"That little scrap of fabric covers what needs to be covered." She looked into Nathan's face. The mischievous twinkle in his eyes immediately made her suspicious. "You know where it is."

"Yep. In my pocket."

"In your *pocket*?"

"You can have it back tomorrow night when you come over for dinner."

This was the first time she'd heard anything about a dinner. "I don't remember receiving an invitation."

"I'm delivering it now. Andre and I would like to cook dinner for you tomorrow evening." He rubbed his upper lip. "To be honest, Andre will do most of the cooking. But I make a great salad and I can open the wine."

Michelle chuckled. "Making a salad is hard, with all that chopping and stuff."

"Yeah, unless you buy the packaged salad."

"That's cheating."

Nathan grinned. "I know."

She liked him. Not only did he make her body sing with a single touch, but she liked his sense of humor and the way he made her laugh.

Both men made her body sing. And she'd be together with them in their apartment tomorrow night. Anything could happen.

Anything at all.

"Is seven all right?" Nathan asked.

"Seven is perfect."

"Then I'll see you tomorrow evening." Lifting her chin with one finger, he tilted up her face for his kiss. "Bye."

"Bye," she said softly.

She watched him leave the office with a sigh. *Such an incredible man.*

Turning back to her desk, she froze when she saw Brent standing in the doorway leading to the kitchen. A dark scowl turned down his mouth.

"What the hell are you doing, Michelle?"

Chapter Eleven

Michelle straightened her spine. She didn't like that condemning tone in Brent's voice. "What do you mean, what am I doing?"

"I saw Nathan kiss you."

"So?"

"Aren't you dating Andre?"

"What does that have to do with my kissing Nathan?"

"Jesus, Michelle, you can't date *both* of them at the same time!"

"Why not?"

His mouth actually dropped open. Michelle didn't think she'd ever seen Brent's mouth drop open. She would've laughed if he didn't look so astonished.

"You aren't…sleeping with both of them, are you?"

"That is none of your business."

"Which means you are. My God, Michelle, you can't do that."

"I don't see why not. I'm not married or engaged. There isn't a rule written somewhere that a woman can't see two men at the same time." She crossed her arms beneath her breasts. "I'm getting really tired of having this same conversation over and over."

"Then stop giving me reasons to start it!"

"I'm not! *You're* the one who keeps bringing it up."

"Hey, hey," a masculine voice said behind her. "What's going on?"

Michelle whirled around. Zach and Jade stood behind her.

The sight of her oldest brother brought the smile back to her face. Despite wanting to strangle Brent, Michelle rushed forward to hug Zach. "Welcome home!" She released Zach and hugged Jade. "You both look wonderful."

"Thanks, sis." He kissed her cheek before reaching out a hand to Brent and drawing him into a hug. "It's good to be home."

Brent released Zach and hugged Jade. "Looks like you spent a lot of time in the sunshine."

"It was incredible. Zach planned a marvelous honeymoon."

"I want to hear all about it." Michelle hooked Jade's arm through hers. "Well, not *all* about it, but the G-rated parts anyway. Let's go in the meeting room and have some tea."

The conversation about Andre and Nathan was over as far as Michelle was concerned, so she saw no reason to tell Zach what she and Brent were discussing. He apparently thought differently.

"So what were you and Brent arguing about when Jade and I came in?"

"Nothing," Michelle hurried to tell him. "Everyone sit down and I'll get the tea."

"Michelle," Zach said in his big brother voice. "I don't like you and Brent arguing. What's up?"

Brent sat at the head of the large table. Michelle stared at him, silently begging him to keep quiet about their argument. She wasn't ready to tell Zach about Andre and Nathan, not until she understood her feelings better.

"It's no big deal, Zach. Michelle and I had a difference of opinion. That's all."

She took back every nasty thought she'd just had about her brother. "Brent and I like to argue, you know that. It keeps the blood flowing. Now sit down. I have sugar cookies too."

"I'll help you, Michelle," Jade said.

"No, no, that's okay. Let me do it. Sit down next to your husband. I'll be right back."

Michelle wanted a few minutes to herself to calm down. Although Brent didn't say anything to Zach about Andre and Nathan, she was still peeved at her older brother for his attitude. He could go out with a different woman every night, but she wasn't supposed to have any desires simply because he still thought of her as his baby sister.

How archaic.

Jade walked into the kitchen as Michelle took four glasses from the cabinet. "What can I do?"

Michelle playfully scowled at her sister-in-law. "I thought I told you to sit by your husband."

"He's talking to Brent about the Cowboys. I'm not into football." She opened the refrigerator and took out a pitcher of tea. "Besides, I'd like a little time with you."

"Sure." Taking cookies from a plastic container, Michelle began arranging them on a plate.

"There was a lot of tension between you and Brent when Zach and I came in. Please don't think I'm trying to interfere. I just want you to know I'm here if you need a woman to talk to." She shrugged one shoulder. "I know technically I'm old enough to be your mother."

"Hardly, unless you had me at fourteen."

"Fourteen isn't too young to have a child." Stepping closer, Jade laid her hand on top of Michelle's. "I know you and Breanna have become close and I'm glad about that, but I'm here too. If you want me to be."

How lucky that her brother had found such an amazing woman. Michelle hugged Jade fiercely. "Thank you. I know you're here for me and I appreciate that so much." She drew back and looked into Jade's face. "My brother hit the jackpot when he found you."

A becoming blush turned Jade's cheeks pink. "I feel the same way about him. I hope you and Brent find someone just as special soon."

The images of Andre and Nathan flashed through Michelle's mind. She'd already found two very special men. Now all she had to do was choose between them.

She had no idea how she would do that.

* * * * *

Nathan leaned over the pot of steaming red sauce and inhaled deeply. "Man, that smells good."

"Of course it does," Andre said with a grin. "I made it."

"You are an excellent cook." He ran his hand down Andre's back and over his buttocks. "As well as being excellent at other things."

"You must be referring to our little…episode in the bedroom earlier."

"We said we wouldn't make love today, that we'd wait for Michelle."

Andre kissed him. "I couldn't resist when I knew you were in the shower."

Nathan had walked into the bedroom after showering to find Andre naked on the bed, slowly stroking his firm cock. It took him two seconds to join his lover on the bed.

"You smell so good," Andre had whispered in his ear while palming Nathan's hardening penis. He slid his lips down Nathan's neck to his chest, stopping to lap at each nipple. "Do you taste as good as you smell?"

"Find out," Nathan had said, pushing his lover's head toward his groin.

"First things first."

Rolling Nathan to his back, Andre had spread Nathan's buttocks and driven his tongue deep inside. Nathan moaned and arched his back, lifting his ass closer to Andre's talented tongue. Andre licked, stroked, darted inside again.

"Love it when you lick my ass," Nathan said, his voice rough.

Andre answered with a murmur against the sensitive flesh. Nathan was on the verge of coming when Andre tugged him to his back and took Nathan's cock in his mouth. Nathan lay still for several moments, enjoying the pleasant sensations shooting through his body, before deciding it wasn't enough for him to accept pleasure without giving in return. He'd moved around on the bed until he could suck Andre's shaft too. They'd come within seconds of each other.

"Besides," Andre said, drawing Nathan back into the present, "neither of us will have any problem getting hard again for Michelle."

"We can't take it for granted that she'll have sex with both of us."

Andre laid the wooden spatula in the spoon rest on the stove. "I don't take anything for granted, but I know how she feels about us. I know how hot she was with me and you told me she was just as hot with you. My talking on the phone about a threesome turned her on."

"It certainly did. Her pussy was so wet, it almost dripped."

"God, it's sweet. Have you ever tasted a sweeter pussy?"

"No." Nathan pressed his palm against his burgeoning cock. "And we'd better stop talking about it or I'll need another blowjob."

Andre kissed him again. "I'm game anytime."

"Tempting, but no. I want to wait for Michelle."

"If I can't suck you off, you can help me cook."

"That's a hell of a choice, man."

Andre grinned. "You can always change your mind."

"You're insatiable, do you know that?"

"And damn proud of it."

"So am I." Nathan picked up the spatula and licked off a generous drop of Andre's red sauce. "God, that's good. We could eat this poured over bread and it would be great."

"That's not what I have in mind." Taking the spatula from Nathan's hand, Andre laid it in the sink. "You can start the pasta while I cut up the chicken."

"Slave driver," Nathan muttered.

Andre palmed Nathan's balls and gently squeezed them. "I'll reward you later…with Michelle."

* * * * *

Michelle drummed her fingertips on the steering wheel, trying to work up the courage to walk to Andre and Nathan's door. She shouldn't be so nervous. It was only dinner. They wouldn't do anything she didn't want them to do. If she decided to have dinner with the men, spend some time with them then go home, they wouldn't object. She knew that.

But she didn't want to simply have dinner and go home. She wanted to make love to them. Both of them. Together. All at once.

She didn't know how to bring up the idea of a threesome. Michelle couldn't see herself blurting out, "Hey, guys, let's all fuck."

Nope, that wouldn't be cool at all.

Things will progress the way they're supposed to. Just let everything happen in its own time.

The pep talk helped her relax. Michelle reached for her purse on the seat. Blowing out a breath, she took the keys from the ignition and left her car.

Nathan opened the door after her knock. He smiled. "Hi."

"Hi. Am I early?"

"You're right on time, no matter what time it is." Taking her hand, he drew her into the apartment. Once he shut the door, he kissed her softly. "I'm glad you're here." His gaze slowly traveled over her. "You look beautiful."

"Thanks."

Michelle had worried about what to wear, as she always did before a date. Nathan had liked the skirt she wore yesterday, so she opted for another one. Swirls of purple, teal and black decorated the fabric. She'd topped the skirt with a simple scooped-neck teal T-shirt.

Beneath her clothes, she wore a skimpy purple bra and thong set she'd bought this afternoon.

"Whatever Andre is cooking smells wonderful."

"It is. You are in for a major treat." He took her purse and laid it on the coffee table. "How about a glass of wine before dinner?"

"I'd like that."

He twined their fingers together and led her to the kitchen. Michelle liked her hand in his. *I feel so close to Nathan, as if we belong together. He has to be the one.*

They stepped into the kitchen. One look at Andre had her heart skittering in her chest.

She no longer doubted that she was equally attracted to both men. Which was crazy. She couldn't fall in love with two men. Not only did society frown on having more than one partner, she doubted if her family and friends would agree to it. Especially Brent. She could hear him ranting now.

Andre turned his head and smiled at her. "Good evening."

"Good evening. I told Nathan that something smells wonderful."

"A pasta dish with chicken. I hope you enjoy it." He walked over and handed her a glass of red wine. "Sit down and enjoy your wine while Nathan and I finish dinner."

"Can I help?"

Andre gave her a gentle kiss. "You are our guest. We wish to wait on you."

Two kisses from two men in less than a minute. While soft and gentle, they were powerful enough to pucker her nipples. She saw Andre's gaze drop to her breasts. A slow smile turned up the corner of his mouth. He knew exactly how that kiss had affected her.

Michelle sat at the table. She took a sip of the hearty wine as she watched the men move around the kitchen, finishing the dinner preparations. It was obvious they were used to working together. She enjoyed watching them easily pass each other while Andre took a dish from the oven and Nathan removed the salad from the refrigerator. Both men had to bend over to complete their tasks. Both men wore tight jeans that molded over their buttocks.

The view was incredible.

Nathan set the bowl of salad on the table. "Be right back," he said, winking at her.

Alone with Andre, she rose from the table and walked over to him. He topped the dish he'd removed from the oven with grated cheese, then replaced it in the oven. "Are you sure I can't help?"

"I am sure." He closed the door and leaned against the cabinet, arms crossed over his chest. "Everything is under control."

"That's good, 'cause to be honest, I'm not a very good cook."

"Oh?"

"Zach and Brent are wonderful cooks. I don't know what happened to me."

"You have talents in other areas. I have seen the flowers at your business and your lovely home. You make things beautiful."

His compliment pleased her. "Thank you."

"Perhaps you will help Nathan and me decorate our home when we find the house we want."

"Are you sure y'all should buy a house together? What if one of you falls in love and wants to get married? You'd have to buy him out, or he'd have to buy you out."

"We do not worry about that."

"Surely you don't think you'll live with Nathan forever."

The sound of a click drew her attention away from Andre. Michelle turned her head to see Nathan standing in the doorway, his camera at his eye. She groaned. "You didn't."

"I did." Lowering the camera, he grinned. "I couldn't resist."

"Nathan rarely lets a day go by without taking a picture."

"Take pictures of Andre, not me."

"I have lots of pictures of Andre." Nathan raised the camera to his eye again. "I want more of you."

"I'm not even posing!"

"I don't want posing." *Click.* "Natural is much better."

She laughed when he clicked the shutter again. "Nathan, stop!"

"Nope." *Click.* "Andre, put your arms around her."

Andre stepped behind her, wrapped his arms around her waist and rested his chin on her shoulder. "Like this?"

"Perfect." *Click.* "Smile for me, Michelle."

Leaning back against Andre, she crossed her arms over his. Instead of smiling as Nathan had requested, she turned her head and kissed Andre's cheek.

Click. "Got it."

"Let me take one of the two of you," Andre said.

"Sure." Nathan handed his camera to Andre, then took Michelle's hand. He sat in a chair at the table and tugged her onto his lap. "Snap away."

Michelle wrapped her arms around Nathan's neck. If he wanted pictures of her, she'd give him a show. She rested her forehead against his and smiled.

Click. "Beautiful," Andre said. "We must take many pictures tonight."

"Sounds good to me," Nathan said softly. Cradling her jaw in his hand, he kissed her. One kiss turned into two, then three. Sighing softly, Michelle relaxed in his arms and returned his slow, drugging kisses.

Click.

The sound of the camera shutter snapped her back to reality. She'd completely lost herself in Nathan's kisses and forgotten Andre was in the room, much less that he held a camera. Standing, she straightened her skirt and top. "Okay, enough of that. When do we eat?"

Andre glanced at the timer on the stove. "The pasta will be done in five minutes. Shall we start with the salad?"

* * * * *

Michelle pushed her plate away from her so she wouldn't be tempted to take a third helping of pasta. Andre's dish was the most sinful thing she'd ever tasted. "I just gained at least fifteen pounds."

Andre chuckled. "I doubt that. But if you did, it will only make you more beautiful."

"You keep heaping on the charm, I may believe you." She stood and reached for Nathan's empty plate. "Y'all cooked, I'll clean."

"Oh, no," Nathan said, covering her hand with his. "No cleaning. Guests don't clean."

"Come on, guys, I'm not a guest."

"You are to us." Nathan stood and took her plate from her hands. "Go in the living room with Andre. I'll take care of this."

"Unless you would rather have dessert now," Andre said.

"I don't have room for dessert."

"Then we will have it later."

She let Andre lead her into the living room. He sat on the couch and coaxed her down beside him, wrapping one arm around her shoulders. "Is this not better than washing dishes?"

"Let me think about it. Sitting next to a hunky man or scraping plates." She tapped her chin with one finger. "Wow, that's a tough one."

"Perhaps I can make it easier for you."

"What do you have in mind?"

He picked up a tendril of hair from her shoulder and wrapped it around his finger. "I thought we might share some kisses before Nathan joins us."

Michelle liked that idea a lot. "I think I could be persuaded to share some kisses."

He tilted up her chin and covered her lips with his. She sighed into his mouth. Andre and Nathan were wonderful kissers. She'd never be able to choose which one was the best.

She didn't want to choose. She wanted both of them.

Andre kissed her cheek before moving back. "Nathan doesn't know what he is missing." He touched her bottom lip with his thumb. "Would you like music?"

"That would be nice."

Andre picked up the remote and pressed a button. Pachelbel's "Canon" drifted through the room. Michelle smiled. "I love this song. It's so beautiful."

"Do you like classical music?"

"Some. I like a little of every kind of music. My favorite is classic rock."

"That is something you and Nathan have in common. He and I sometimes argue over whose turn it is to play the stereo."

"Arguing is no fun."

"I agree." His eyes turned smoky, heated. He ran his thumb over her lip again. "I would much rather make love."

Michelle sank into his arms when he kissed her. Andre's earlier kisses had been sweet and loving. These were passionate, demanding, raising her blood pressure and desire.

She moaned when he cradled her breast. He molded her flesh to his palm, his thumb teased her nipple into a hard point. She parted her lips when his tongue touched them. Pulling her closer to him, he deepened the kisses while he continued to caress her breast.

Michelle whimpered with pleasure.

She jerked in surprise when she felt Nathan press up against her back. Pulling away from Andre, she looked at Nathan over her shoulder.

"Don't stop," Nathan said, his voice raspy. "I want to watch Andre touch you."

She gazed at one man, then the other, trying to decide if she should act on her feelings. Her eyes drifted closed when Andre cupped her breast again. A moment later, she felt a hand on her other breast. She opened her eyes to see each man was touching her.

She'd never seen anything so exciting.

"Stay with us, Michelle," Andre whispered in her ear. "Let us pleasure you tonight."

Chapter Twelve

ಐ

It seemed like a dream when the men took her hands and pulled her to her feet. Andre kissed her first, then Nathan. Still holding her hands, they led her to a bedroom. Michelle didn't know if it was Andre's or Nathan's room, and she didn't care. All she wanted was to put out the fire raging in her veins.

She had mere moments to take in the masculine furnishings before Nathan directed her to the king-sized bed. He gently pushed on her shoulders until she sat on the edge. A single lamp burned on the nightstand. He turned it off as Andre lit candles around the room.

"Andre said you like candles."

"I do." Her voice came out hoarse. Her clit throbbed, her womb contracted with every breath she took. She'd never felt desire so strongly, so deeply. Knowing these men—*both* these men—were going to make love to her left her weak with wanting.

Three swipes across her clit and she'd come.

Nathan stood in front of her while Andre finished lighting the candles. Her gaze slowly traveled down his body to his crotch. The outline of his erect cock through his jeans caused her to swallow hard.

She didn't know whether to undress or wait for a cue from them. She longed to be naked and sandwiched between those two hard bodies.

The thought made her shiver.

Andre came to the bed. Looking into her eyes, he began unbuttoning his shirt. Once it hit the floor, Nathan tugged off his pullover and dropped it on top of Andre's shirt. Michelle clenched her fists to keep from reaching out and caressing those firm male chests, sliding her fingertips across hard dark nipples. Her own nipples beaded in response to her thoughts.

Belts came off next. Jeans were unfastened. Her breathing grew heavier as she watched each man push his jeans over his hips. Stiff cocks stood straight up, almost begging for attention.

Hands or mouth. She didn't know which one to use first on them.

The decision was taken from her when Andre dropped to his knees. He slid her skirt farther up her legs. "Open for me," he whispered.

Spreading her legs, Michelle leaned back and braced herself with her palms. She lifted her hips when he grasped the waistband of her thong. He pulled it off and dropped it on top of his and Nathan's clothing.

"This night is for you, Michelle." He kissed her knee. "Whatever you want." Another kiss fell on the inside of her thigh. "Anything you want." The tip of his tongue tickled the sensitive spot between thigh and pelvis. "However you want it." He swiped his tongue across her clit. "Just tell us what you want and we'll do it."

Moaning, Michelle arched her hips and spread her legs even wider. "That. Lick my pussy. I want to come."

Nathan climbed on the bed behind her. "That's what we want too, for you to come again and again." She leaned back on his chest as he palmed her breasts. "How about if I play with your nipples while Andre licks you?"

"Mmm, yes."

A moment later, her top and bra had joined the pile of clothing on the floor. Nathan caressed her breasts, lifting and squeezing the full globes. He flicked her nipples with his thumbs, pinched them with thumbs and forefingers. Between the stimulation on her nipples and her clit, Michelle knew an orgasm would hit her quickly.

She grabbed handfuls of Andre's hair when the climax took her. "*Ohhhhhhhhh!*" He continued to lick her clit, sending a smaller, less intense, orgasm thundering through her body. She would've collapsed on the bed if Nathan hadn't been behind her. He continued to rub her nipples, keeping the stimulation flooding her body.

Nathan nipped her earlobe. "God, you're hot."

"Yeah," Andre said in a guttural voice. He wiped her juices from his chin. "I love how quickly you come."

"I don't…" She had to stop and take a breath. "I don't usually come so quickly."

Andre grinned wickedly. "So Nathan and I are doing something right, yes?"

Michelle chuckled weakly. "You could say that, yeah."

"Excellent." He touched her tender clit with the pad of his thumb. "We want to give you the most pleasure you've ever received."

A sharp tweak of her nipples made Michelle gasp. Nathan nipped her earlobe again, then drove his tongue into her ear. Goose bumps scattered across her skin. "Have you ever been with two men, Michelle?"

She shook her head.

"Ever fantasized about it?"

"Yes," she whispered.

Andre began to lick her pussy again. Michelle propped her feet on the bed and let her legs fall open.

"That's the way," Nathan said, still massaging her nipples. "Show us what you like, what you want. It's all about your pleasure."

She could feel Nathan's hard cock pressed against her lower back. "What-what about you?"

His chuckle sounded devilish. "Andre and I will find pleasure too, believe me. But our main concern is *you* and what pleases you."

"What if… Oh!" She drew in a sharp breath when Andre suckled her clit. "What if I want to do something to you or Andre?"

"Name it."

"I want to suck someone's cock."

"Pick one of us."

How was she supposed to pick someone when she couldn't even *think*? Andre's talented tongue and Nathan's incredible fingers were driving her toward another orgasm.

She never would have believed her body could be capable of such sensations.

Nathan released one nipple and caressed her lower lip. "I've already come in your mouth. How about if you suck on Andre?"

Michelle nodded. "Just-just a sec. I'm close…"

"Fuck her with your fingers, Andre."

No sooner had Andre done as Nathan instructed than Michelle shivered. She bit her bottom lip to keep from crying out.

"Still want a cock in your mouth?" Nathan asked in her ear.

Despite feeling as weak as a brand-new puppy, Michelle laughed. "I don't have the strength to breathe, much less do anything else." She pushed her hair back from her forehead. "I know I need to."

"You don't *need* to do anything," Andre said.

"But that isn't fair. I've come twice. You and Nathan haven't come once."

"We will." Nathan squeezed her nipples again. "But first, how about a massage?"

"That'll put me to sleep."

"I doubt that." He shifted behind her and Michelle lay back on the bed. Nathan lowered his head and kissed her. "Roll over on your stomach."

With Nathan's help since her strength hadn't yet returned, Michelle rolled to her stomach in the middle of the large bed. Andre removed her skirt and shoes, leaving her as naked as the two men. Closing her eyes, she lowered her forehead to her crossed arms.

She heard a drawer open and close. A bottle top flipped open. Warm, slick hands touched her lower back. She didn't know if Nathan or Andre touched her, nor did she care. The hands moved over her buttocks and down her legs, then slowly made the return journey. She sighed contentedly.

Another set of hands began massaging her shoulders. The bed dipped as one of the men moved. Michelle lifted her head. Andre knelt in front of her, his legs spread wide, his hard cock less than six inches from her mouth.

Any weakness she'd experienced from her orgasms completely vanished.

She reached out and cupped his tight balls in her palm. His breathing grew heavier, but he didn't stop the massage. His hands moved over her shoulders and down her back to the dip of her waist. Nathan continued to rub her legs and buttocks. Michelle began her own massage of Andre's shaft, her fingers sliding up and down the velvety skin. He was big, possibly the biggest she'd ever touched.

She looked up into Andre's eyes and saw the blaze of desire. Scooting closer to him, she took the plum-shaped head between her lips. Andre hissed. Parting her lips wider, she took more of him into her mouth. Nathan's hands stilled on her lower body. She assumed that meant he was watching her. Releasing Andre's shaft, she licked her lips before taking him in her mouth again. She moved slowly, sliding her mouth forward until her nose touched his pubic hair. Andre didn't move. She drew back just as slowly to the head, then repeated the path.

He smelled so good…different from Nathan, but no less appealing. Musk and man. An arousing combination.

She felt Nathan's fingers between her thighs. Michelle rose to her knees and spread her legs.

"That's good, baby," Nathan rasped. "Let me play with this sweet pussy."

He pushed a finger inside her. She whimpered and spread her legs a bit more. She'd had two potent orgasms, but still wanted more.

A second finger joined the first, then a third. Nathan drove them in and out of her channel, caressing her G-spot, as Andre pushed his cock farther into her mouth.

She moaned when Nathan licked her anus. His fingers kept performing their magic inside her while his tongue stroked her. Pleasure grew, expanded, flowed through her. It crested when Nathan thrust his tongue into her ass.

The waves were still shimmering through her body when Nathan slid his cock inside her pussy. Andre gathered her hair in one fist and began fucking her mouth…gently at first, but he picked up speed as Nathan's lunges quickened.

Andre came first, his salty cum filling her mouth and sliding down her throat. Nathan soon followed, gripping her hips and groaning loudly. The intensity of her last orgasm sapped any strength Michelle had left. Her legs gave out and she fell to the bed. She lay still, heart pounding, fighting for breath.

Andre pushed her hair back from her face. "Are you all right?"

"No. I'm wiped. I'll never have sex again."

Nathan kissed each buttock, the small of her back, between her shoulder blades. "You can rest for a few minutes before we start all over again."

Laughter burst from her throat. She rolled to her back to see him resting on one elbow beside her, his eyes twinkling with amusement. "What makes you think I can do anything else?"

"Because Andre and I are studs."

"I'll agree with that."

"And because you make us feel things we've never felt with a woman," Andre said as he stretched out beside her. He cradled one breast in his palm. "We want many nights with you just like this."

"I'll second that." Nathan cupped her other breast and whisked his thumb across the nipple. "You're lovely, sexy and very desirable."

He kissed her. Michelle sighed and wrapped her arms around his neck. He continued to play with her breast while Andre caressed the other one. They tugged the nipples, squeezed the mounds, pushed them together and upward. Her nipples would probably be sore tomorrow with all this attention.

Michelle didn't care.

As soon as Nathan lifted his lips from hers, Andre kissed her. He rolled to his back, tugging her along with him. She lay on top of him, her legs on either side of his hips.

She tunneled her fingers into Andre's thick mane. She loved touching his hair, feeling the strands flow through her fingers. "Nathan said we would wait a few minutes."

"Nathan lied."

Andre's kisses grew deeper, bolder. He shifted beneath her, rubbing his hardening flesh against her stomach. Nathan's fingers began to probe her feminine lips again. He dipped between the folds and spread her cream over her anus. His touch felt wonderful, but fingers weren't enough. She wanted more.

Rising to her knees, Michelle gripped Andre's rod and took him inside her body. She looked at Nathan over her shoulder. He stared at the place where she and Andre were joined. Slowly, he raised his gaze to hers. Looking in her eyes, he pushed a finger into her ass. She arched back at his hand, driving his finger deeper inside her.

"Do you want me here?"

She nodded.

"Let me watch you fuck Andre first."

Michelle braced her hands on Andre's shoulders and began to ride his shaft. He clutched her waist, meeting each of her movements. Slow thrusts soon turned to fast pounding.

"My God, this looks good," Nathan growled.

She glanced over her shoulder again. Nathan opened the bottle of oil and poured a generous amount in his palm. He spread it over his cock, concentrating on the head.

"Andre, pull her down to your chest."

Whimpering in anticipation, Michelle closed her eyes. Andre gripped her buttocks and pulled them apart. The tip of Nathan's shaft touched her anus. Even though she wanted this, she tightened at the unfamiliar contact.

"Relax, baby," Nathan crooned. "I won't hurt you."

Andre cradled her face and kissed her softly, sweetly. Michelle sighed and relaxed against him. This time when Nathan touched her, she arched her hips back at him.

"Just like that, baby." He pressed forward. Michelle felt the head slip inside her. "Mmm, nice and tight."

She lowered her face to Andre's neck. *You want this, Michelle. You've wanted this for a long time.* Another inch slid inside her, then another. She took a breath. Nathan pushed forward as she released it.

He kissed her nape. "I'm all the way in, Michelle."

"I know."

"Everything okay?"

"It will be when you start fucking me."

His chuckle vibrated against her back. "Whatever the lady wants."

He drew out, then pushed in again. Once, twice, he thrust into her ass before Andre began to move also. The two men established a rhythm—in, out, in, out, slow, fast, slow, fast.

"You still okay, Michelle?" Andre asked.

"Yessssss." She pushed up on her hands and looked at him. "It feels so good."

She was surrounded by hard muscles and sweaty flesh. Her own arousal filled her nostrils. She inhaled deeply, loving her scent mixed with Andre's and Nathan's.

Nathan thrust faster. Sandwiched between the two men, she couldn't move—she could only accept what they gave her. Kisses fell on her forehead, her shoulder blade, her neck. She didn't know which man kissed what, and didn't care. All that mattered was the pleasure building inside her body again.

Andre slid one hand between them and tweaked her nipple. That tiny bit of extra stimulation did it for her. Michelle groaned loudly as the orgasm exploded in her clit and traveled through every part of her body.

Andre moaned first, followed closely by Nathan, who stretched out on top of her, covering her body with his. Both men's cocks remained nestled inside her.

Michelle had no idea how long they lay together. Her heart had finally stopped pounding, but her mouth was so dry she didn't think she could speak.

"Would you like a drink?" Nathan asked close to her ear.

"Please," she croaked.

"I'll move as soon as I can get my legs to work."

"I am in no hurry," Andre said. "I like having Michelle on top of me."

"She can stay there. I'll get our drinks."

Michelle groaned softly when Nathan pulled out of her. He caressed each buttock before climbing down from the bed. She could feel his essence leaking from her anus.

"I think I'd better get cleaned up."

"The bathroom is to the right."

She kissed Andre and rose from the bed on trembling legs. Once alone in the bathroom, she leaned against the closed door for support and blew out a breath. *Wow. What an intense experience*. She'd fantasized about being with two men but had no idea the reality would top her fantasies. She didn't know if it would be as mind-boggling with two different men or if only Andre and Nathan could affect her so strongly.

She suspected the latter.

Every minute with them, her feelings deepened. If she had to choose right now which man to be with, she couldn't. She cared too much for both of them.

But she *did* have to choose—she knew that. She couldn't continue to see both men. It wasn't fair to her heart, and it wasn't fair to them. Nathan had already told her he loved her. Andre hadn't said the words yet, but she suspected his feelings were just as strong as Nathan's. The way he looked at her, touched her, proved that.

She didn't have to make a decision tonight. She'd spend a bit more time with them, then go home. Zach and Jade had invited her to their house for dinner tomorrow night. That would still give her all day tomorrow to herself, to think about what she wanted to do about the two sexy men in the next room.

* * * * *

Nathan walked back into the bedroom with a huge glass of iced tea to see Andre with his eyes closed, propped up by several pillows. One leg was straight, the other bent. His cock lay relaxed against his thigh, glistening with Michelle's juices.

The sight was too tempting. Nathan set the glass on the nightstand, bent over and took Andre's penis in his mouth.

"Mmm." Andre arched his hips. "Nice."

Nathan pulled his lover's shaft deeper into his mouth and felt him begin to harden. He'd always loved how quickly Andre could get hard again after sex.

Andre touched his head. "You'd better stop unless you want Michelle to see you."

"Don't want to stop." He pulled Andre's cock into his mouth again, then licked his balls. "Love the way your dick tastes after you've fucked her."

"Kiss me."

Nathan leaned forward and took Andre's mouth in a deep kiss. He groaned when Andre palmed his rod and stroked it. A few more moments of kissing and fondling and they'd both have hard cocks again.

Andre was breathing heavily when Nathan ended the kiss. "Damn, I love kissing you."

"The feeling is mutual." Andre kissed Nathan again. "It was hot, wasn't it? Both of us fucking her at the same time. Next time I get her ass."

"Deal." He picked up the glass of tea. "Everything about tonight has been hot." He took a large gulp before handing the glass to Andre. "She's perfect for us."

"So when do we tell her we're a couple?"

Nathan rubbed the stubble on his upper lip. "Not yet. This was the first time the three of us have been together, the first time she's been with two men. I don't want to bombard her with too much at once."

"We have to tell her soon. I don't want to hide anything from her. It was hard to keep from touching you."

"Me too."

Nathan heard the bathroom door open. "She's coming back."

It pleased Nathan to see Michelle walk back into the bedroom still naked. She could've wrapped a towel around herself or taken one of their robes off the back of the door.

Instead, she walked toward the bed, breasts thrust forward, hips swaying.

She stopped by Andre and took the glass of tea from him. Nathan watched her gaze move from him to Andre and back again. She looked at their faces first, then their laps.

The little sex goddess was still hungry. Good.

"Would you rather have wine?" he asked.

"No, this is fine." She set the glass on the nightstand. "Thank you both. For everything."

"That sounds suspiciously like a goodbye."

"It is. I have to go home."

"Why?" Andre asked.

"Why? Well, because."

"That is not a good reason."

She frowned at Andre. "I can't stay all night."

"Yes, you can." Andre took her hand and urged her closer to the bed. "Nathan and I are not through with you."

She landed on the bed on her knees. "Guys, I can't do any more. Really. I've used up my orgasm quota for tonight. I've used it up for the next two *weeks*."

"*We* haven't." Nathan pulled one nipple between his lips and suckled. He was rewarded by Michelle's soft gasp. "And I'll bet we can find another orgasm for you. Maybe even two."

She didn't resist when he tugged her down on the bed between him and Andre.

Chapter Thirteen

ഇ

Michelle jumped when Zach leaned down and peered into her face. "Where are you, sis?"

In bed with Andre and Nathan. Clearing her throat, she gestured at the vegetables surrounding the cutting board. "Right here in your kitchen, chopping veggies for the salad. It's my special talent since I can't cook."

"You could cook if you tried."

"I don't want to burn down my house." She scraped the lettuce into a large glass bowl and picked up a dark red tomato. "I know my limits."

"I think you're chicken."

"No, just realistic. I've tried a hundred different dishes. They all end up in the garbage disposal. I simply don't have the knack."

"I'll be glad to give you cooking lessons. I'll bet Jade would too. She's a great cook."

Michelle knew Jade and Zach often divided up the kitchen duties and prepared meals together. They were so much in love, a person would never be able to tell they'd gone through crushing heartache before they married. Jade had been worried that the ten-year difference in their ages would come back to haunt Zach someday. Plus the fact that she couldn't have any more children. It had taken Zach's total commitment to her to convince Jade that he loved her, despite being younger than she. Their ages hadn't mattered to him, nor the lack of children. If they ever decided a child would add to their lives, they'd talked about hiring a surrogate or adopting.

He loved his wife totally, completely. That's the kind of love Michelle wanted. She had no doubt she could have that kind of love with Andre or Nathan.

She didn't know which man to pick.

Housework always helped her think. Michelle had cleaned out closets today while she tried to decide what to do. She couldn't have a future with both men but she couldn't choose one. They were alike, yet different. She loved Andre's charm, his consideration, his old-world manners. She loved Nathan's sense of humor, his talent with a camera, the way he made her feel safe. Of course, both of them were gorgeous and incredible lovers.

She wished she could combine the two men into one. End of her problem.

"Sis, hand me the egg noodles. They're in the cabinet above your head."

"Sure." Michelle wiped her hands on a dishcloth and opened the cabinet. Zach was preparing his famous beef stroganoff for dinner at Jade's request. It was the first meal he'd prepared for her when they were dating. Since Jade was such a romantic, Michelle had no doubt that her sister-in-law requested the dish often.

"I noticed Jade and Breanna disappeared as soon as we started fixing supper."

Zach chuckled. "I don't mind. Jade hasn't seen her daughter in three weeks. I'm sure they have a lot to catch up on."

"Where's Brent?"

"On the patio."

Michelle looked out the kitchen window. Brent sat in one of the lounge chairs, nursing a beer. "Is he okay?"

"I don't know. He said he's fine, but I think something's wrong. He's moody, even more than usual." Zach tore open the bag of noodles and dumped them into boiling water. "I wish he'd confide in me. That's what brothers are for."

The perfect opening. Michelle took a sip of her Coke before facing her brother. "Can I talk to you?"

"Yeah." He gave the noodles a stir and laid the wooden spoon on the stove. "What's up?"

"I...have a problem."

Zach leaned back against the counter. "I'm listening."

"Our new escorts, Andre and Nathan. You haven't met them yet, have you?"

"Not yet. I'll meet them tomorrow night."

Michelle had forgotten about the meeting. All the escorts would be at the office tomorrow evening to meet with the three owners of Coopers' Companions and Jade. Most of the guys had already met Jade, but Zach wanted all their escorts to know her.

"I, uh, sorta went out with them."

"Define 'sorta'."

"I dated Andre first, then Nathan."

Zach said nothing. He stood still and looked at her.

"I like both of them. I really, really like both of them."

"So your problem is what?"

"Zach, I like *both* of them. I want both of them. I can't be involved with two men."

"Then you'll have to choose between them."

"I *can't*! They're both such special men."

Zach stepped over to the stove and stirred the noodles. "I don't know what you want me to say, Chelle."

"Tell me what to do."

"Is there a reason you can't date both of them? Go out with Andre one time, then Nathan."

Michelle picked up her glass of Coke and swirled the straw through the ice. "It's a little more complicated than that."

"How?"

"We—the three of us—were together last night. In bed."

"Oh." Zach gave the noodles another stir. "Damn, I still have a hard time with you and sex."

"You sound like Brent."

"Heaven forbid." Replacing the spoon on the stove, Zach once again leaned back against the counter. "I've been in a *ménage a trois*, Chelle. More than one, in fact."

Michelle's eyes widened. She had no idea Zach had done something like that. "Two women at once?"

"Sometimes two women, sometimes one woman and another man. It can be very intense. Desire is high, hormones are raging. It's easy to confuse lust for love."

"I'm not the least confused. I know exactly how I feel about them."

"Sounds like you made your decision," he said softly.

It surprised her to realize that Zach was right. She *had* made her decision. She wanted both men in her life. But how did she explain that to her mother, her friends, Brent? Her other brother would hit the roof.

Zach stepped closer to her. "I'm in a... Well, I'd guess you'd call it a non-traditional relationship. There are many, many women involved with younger men, but it's usually reversed. I knew from my first date with Jade that I wanted to be with her the rest of my life. You have to do what's right for you, Chelle. If you want to be involved with *five* men, go for it if it makes you happy."

Michelle hugged him fiercely. She knew Zach would understand. "I love you so much."

"I love you too." He released her and returned to the stove. "Just think about it long and hard before you make any permanent arrangements. You can't legally marry two men. At least, not in Texas."

Marry? Michelle hadn't even thought about marriage. "Uh, that isn't an option any time soon."

"But it may be in the future. The three of you have to talk about it before a suitcase is packed or any furniture moved." He turned off the burner beneath the noodles. "I assume they'll move in with you."

Of course they'd move in with her. She already had a house while they hadn't found one yet. She didn't have a king-sized bed, but they'd slept in one last night. She could sell her queen and use Andre's or Nathan's bed.

Ohmigod, I'm really considering this!

"I'll talk to them tomorrow about moving in with me."

"It's probably a good idea. A try-it-before-you-buy-it thing to see if it's really what you want." He flashed her a grin. "You may not like picking up two pairs of shorts from the floor."

"They don't wear shorts."

"Aw, shit, Chelle, don't tell me stuff like that."

She grinned. "Sorry."

"You don't sound the least bit sorry." Zach poured the noodles into a metal colander in the sink to rinse. "I think you enjoy getting the best of me."

She did enjoy it for it happened so rarely. Grinning to herself, she picked up the knife and reached for the package of celery. "About those *ménages* you were involved in?"

"Yeah?"

"Did you ever…you know, do anything with another guy?"

Zach turned off the hot water and faced her. His mouth quirked at one corner. "There are some things you don't need to know, Chelle."

* * * * *

Michelle rinsed the glass and placed it in the dishwasher. As soon as she finished straightening up the kitchen, she wanted to get Andre and Nathan alone to talk to them.

Zach had struck up a conversation with the two men shortly after the meeting had ended. Between clearing the table and putting away snacks and drinks, Michelle hadn't had the chance to hear what they were saying. She didn't think Zach was drilling the two men—that was more Brent's style. Still, she'd like to know what they were saying.

"Last of the glasses," Jade said, setting two next to the sink. "I'll wipe off the table and then we're done."

"Thanks."

She took a washcloth from the drawer, but held it instead of wetting it. "Can we talk?"

"Sure." Michelle closed the dishwasher. "Is something wrong?"

"Zach told me about your two men."

Michelle closed her eyes. She should've known Zach would confide in his wife. Jade had to know about Andre and Nathan, but Michelle had hoped for a little more time to figure out how to break it to everyone. She looked back at her sister-in-law. "I suppose you think I'm crazy."

"Actually, I think you're brave to do something you want despite what other people may say."

Her praise touched Michelle. She cared deeply for Jade and wanted her approval.

"It's obvious Andre and Nathan care a great deal for you. They stared at you all through the meeting."

"I care a great deal for them too."

"Then you should do what makes you happy." She leaned closer to Michelle. Her eyes twinkled with devilment. "I think two hunks in bed at the same time would make you *very* happy."

Michelle grinned. "Only once so far, but it was incredible."

"What was incredible?" Zach asked, stepping behind his wife.

"Girl talk, bro."

"In other words, none of my business."

"Right."

"I never get to do anything fun." He slipped his arms around Jade's waist. "Ready to go? Brent said he'd lock up. He's still talking to some of the guys."

"Okay. Michelle, do you mind?"

"Of course not. I'll wipe off the table. Oh, wait. I've been meaning to ask you something, Jade. Have you lost weight?"

Smiling, Jade pressed her hands against her flat stomach. "Fourteen pounds! I think it was all that walking we did on our honeymoon."

"Walking." Zach chuckled. "Yeah, right. Walking."

Jade looked at him over her shoulder. "We *did* do a lot of walking."

"We did a lot of other things too," he said, nuzzling Jade's ear.

Michelle waved her hand at them. "Go home. I don't want to hear about y'all making love three times a day."

Zach grinned. "Sometimes more than three."

"I'll hurt him later, Michelle, I promise."

"Please do."

Michelle watched them walk out of the kitchen hand in hand before turning her attention back to the meeting room. Her gaze met Andre's. He winked at her. That simple gesture made her heart race.

She motioned for him to come to her. He said something to Peter, who sat next to him at the table, then rose from his chair and walked into the kitchen. He smiled. "Hi."

"Hi," she said, returning his smile. "Did you have a good talk with Zach?"

"Yes, I did. He is a very intelligent man. I like him."

"Good. I'm glad." She clasped her hands together at her waist. "Do you remember how to get to my house?"

He nodded.

"Will you and Nathan come by later? I'd like to talk to both of you."

"Is something wrong?"

"I'll tell you later, okay?"

"Of course. We will come by as soon as we leave here."

* * * * *

Nathan maneuvered the SUV around a slow-moving pickup. "She's going to break up with us."

Andre slumped down in the passenger seat. He didn't want to think of that possibility but it could happen. Michelle had probably decided she couldn't be involved with two men. Instead of disappointing one of them, she was going to break off with both of them.

Damn it.

"You don't know that, Nathan."

"Then why wouldn't she tell you what she wanted to talk about?"

"Her brother was five feet away from us."

"She could've given you a hint, at least told you there wasn't anything wrong."

"There *isn't* anything wrong. There can't be." Andre straightened and turned toward Nathan. "I won't lose her. I love her."

"I love her too."

"So if she tries to end it with us, we'll have to show her how good we are together, how much we have in common."

161

"I don't think having things in common is the problem. How many women would be willing to live with two men? Especially when she finds out those two men love each other."

"Michelle is a modern woman. She'll accept our relationship."

"I hope you're right, man."

* * * * *

Michelle peeked out the kitchen window when she heard Nathan's SUV pull into her driveway. She watched both men climb out of the vehicle and head toward her front door. Having this conversation wouldn't be easy. Even though she wanted to be with both Andre and Nathan, Zach was right that certain…ground rules had to be established. It was way too soon to talk about marriage, yet there were other things the three of them had to discuss.

She opened the door before either man had the chance to ring the doorbell. "Hi. Come in."

She led the way into the living room, where she'd set up a bottle of white wine and three glasses. After motioning for them to sit on the couch, she perched on the edge of the armchair. "Andre, will you pour the wine please?"

Silently, Andre uncorked the bottle and poured a small amount into all three glasses. He handed one glass to her and Nathan before taking one for himself. "Will Nathan and I need this wine, Michelle?"

"No. At least I hope not."

She had their attention with that statement. "I'm doing this all wrong, aren't I?"

"Michelle," Nathan said, leaning forward and setting his untouched wine back on the coffee table, "just say whatever you want to say."

"But know we aren't giving up." Andre also set his glass on the table. "I love you, Michelle. I don't want to lose you."

It was the first time Andre had mentioned love. Warmth spread through her at those beautiful words. "I don't want to lose you or Nathan either."

"So you didn't bring us here to break up with us?"

Michelle shook her head. "No. I brought you here to ask you to move in with me."

A look of relief flashed through both men's eyes. Michelle held up one hand to stop them from saying anything. "It's crazy for me to be in love with two men, I know that. Yet I can't help the way I feel. I want to be with both of you."

Nathan reached over and took her hand. "We want to be with you too."

"Do you? Will you be happy sharing me with Andre? And I'm not talking about only sex. A couple needs to spend time together. I'll have to divide my time in two."

"Andre and I understand that."

"I hope so. I truly do. I don't know if this will work, but I'm willing to try."

"So are we," Andre said.

She pulled her hand away from Nathan's. It was easier for her to think when he didn't touch her. "There have to be rules."

"Like?" Nathan asked.

"You told me you and Andre aren't much at cleaning house. I won't be a maid. If you live here, you do your part."

"I have no problem with that." Nathan looked at Andre. "Do you?"

"No. And before you mention cooking, you know I love to cook. I will be happy to prepare the meals."

"I'm glad you said that, 'cause I suck at cooking."

Michelle sipped her wine. So far, this had been easy, but she doubted it would remain that way. "What about your jobs? Working as escorts isn't an option. I won't share."

"What if you continued to set us up with women who were not interested in sex, only an escort?" Nathan asked. "It's worked so far."

"I set Andre up with a woman who most definitely wanted sex." She looked at Andre. "I know it's none of my business because it happened before we were involved, but I have to ask this. Did you have sex with Angela Dubois?"

"No, I did not."

She found that hard to believe. She *knew* Angela Dubois. The woman oozed sex appeal and had fucked every one of her escorts that she'd dated. "Don't lie to me to protect my feelings, Andre."

"I am not lying, Michelle. Angela tried to get me into bed. She tried to take me in her kitchen, in fact. But I refused." His eyes softened and she could clearly see love shining in them. "I cannot be with another woman when I am in love with you."

Everything inside her melted at his sweet words. Anything else she'd wanted to talk about fled from her mind. Right now, all she wanted was to be in his arms. And Nathan's. "I think this is where I say something like, 'okay, talk over, let's go to bed'."

Neither man smiled at her joke. Michelle set her glass on the table. "Is something wrong?"

"Michelle, there is something Andre and I need to tell you."

Nathan's tone sounded much too serious. Michelle swallowed a knot of apprehension. "All right."

He looked at Andre. "I don't know how to say it."

"Perhaps we should show her instead of tell her."

Andre cradled Nathan's face in his hands and kissed him.

Chapter Fourteen

ॐ

Michelle stared at the two men as the kiss deepened. She blinked, certain the vision in front of her eyes wasn't real. Andre and Nathan *kissing*? It couldn't be happening. They weren't gay. They'd both made love to her. They'd said they loved her. They couldn't possibly be gay!

"Stop it!"

The kiss ended with a loud *smack*. Both men turned to look at her, worry in their eyes.

"I don't understand," she whispered past the knot in her throat.

Nathan clasped Andre's hand. "Andre and I love each other, Michelle. We fell in love as soon as we met four years ago. We've been together ever since. We're committed to each other."

"But-but you both said you love *me*. How can you be in love and love me too?"

"You love both of us," Andre said. "Why can't we love each other and you too?"

She rubbed her forehead, hoping that would help clear her thoughts. She thought she'd found the perfect men, the ones she wanted to be with for the rest of her life. Instead, she'd been fooled into falling for two men who only wanted men. "You're gay?"

"No," Andre said firmly. "We don't like labels, Michelle. Nathan and I don't consider ourselves gay or straight or bi. We have been involved with both men and women. We enjoy sex with both men and women. That makes us human."

She'd never thought of it that way. Several of her girlfriends had experimented with other women. They preferred sex with men but said they'd enjoyed the experience with other women.

"Have you ever had sex with a woman?" Nathan asked.

"No, of course not."

"Why do you say 'of course not'? Have you ever admired the way a woman looked, the way she moved? Have you ever wondered what it would be like to make love to her?"

She'd done everything he mentioned. She'd never acted on her curiosity, as her girlfriends had, but she'd wondered what it would be like to kiss a woman, caress her, taste her. She nodded.

"Do you think that makes you a lesbian?"

"No. I like sex with men too much to be a lesbian. I guess...I guess it makes me human."

Nathan smiled. "Yeah, it does."

Michelle blew out a breath. Her mind still whirled from learning Andre and Nathan were lovers. "So what does this mean?"

"It means we're all in love and we're going to have a wonderful life together."

"Just like that?"

"Just like that."

"You make it sound so easy."

"It is. We may have a few more hurdles to cross than most couples, but there's nothing we can't handle as long as we love and trust each other."

Love and trust were the most important parts of a relationship. Michelle had always believed that. Still... "What about my family?" she asked, switching her attention to Andre. "What do I tell them?"

"Would you tell them about your sex life if you were involved with only one man?"

"No."

"Then there is no reason to tell them anything. Nathan and I are not ashamed of our love, Michelle, but we do not flaunt it either. There is no reason anyone in your family has to know anything about your sex life."

Andre was right. Anything that went on in her bedroom was no one's business but hers, Andre's and Nathan's. They could do whatever they wanted behind closed doors. She and Nathan, she and Andre, the three of them...or simply Andre and Nathan. Two buff men, naked and sweaty, cocks hard and ready to fill mouths and asses.

Her womb clenched at the thought.

"Your eyes are turning smoky, Michelle," Andre said. "What are you thinking?"

She looked from one man to the other. Honesty was also a big part of a relationship. "About the two of you having sex."

"I had hoped you were thinking of that. Are you curious?"

She nodded.

"Do you want to watch, or participate?"

"Both."

Andre stood and held out his hand to her. "Then make love with us."

Michelle accepted Andre's hand and stood. He held out his other hand to Nathan. She led the way to her bedroom, the two men following behind her.

Releasing the men's hands, she moved to the bedside lamps and switched on both of them. She could light candles, but that wouldn't give her the brightness she desired. "I want to see everything."

"So do we. Andre and I prefer to make love in the light."

She walked back to the men and kissed first Nathan, then Andre. "Take off your clothes."

Andre reached for the hem of her T-shirt. "I believe we should take off yours first."

The shirt disappeared before Michelle had the chance to argue. "Hey, getting naked was *my* idea."

"And a damn good one," Nathan said, unfastening her jeans.

"I meant for you and Andre to get naked first."

"There's two of us and one of you. We can strip you faster."

Michelle couldn't help laughing at Nathan's reasoning. Her laughter ended with a soft shriek when he pushed her down on the bed and attacked her shoes. Andre removed her bra before helping Nathan with her shoes and socks. Less than a minute from the time they started, she sat naked before them.

Michelle leaned back on her elbows. Her being naked while the men were still dressed seemed to be the norm for them. It made her feel wicked and sexy. "I gather y'all have had a lot of experience undressing women."

"More each other than other women. I greatly enjoy undressing Nathan." Andre ran his hand over her right breast. "My God, you have beautiful breasts. I will never get enough of touching them."

Nathan tweaked the other nipple, then drew it into his mouth and suckled. The sensation shot all the way to her toes. "Oh, yes. I do like that." She clasped Andre's wrist and urged him closer. "Two mouths, two nipples."

His lips quirked. "Is that a hint?"

"No, it's a demand. Suck me."

Andre obeyed her command, drawing her nipple deep into his mouth. He licked it, flicked it with the tip of his tongue, sucked it. Nathan repeated the movements on her other nipple, but at different times. When Andre sucked, Nathan licked. When Andre flicked, Nathan sucked. Not only did the sensations shoot down to her toes, they made her toes curl. Michelle closed her eyes and arched her back, greedily taking everything they would give her. Pleasure climbed, receded, climbed again.

Nathan released one nipple but continued to caress it with his fingertips. "I still want to try nipple clamps on you."

The orgasm whooshed through her body so quickly, she barely had time to draw in a breath. She'd been close to coming many times from having her nipples sucked but had never crossed that line into paradise. With two men paying special attention to her breasts and Nathan's naughty suggestion, she not only crossed the line—she high-jumped over it.

"What's this about nipple clamps?" Andre asked.

"Something Michelle and I talked about. She said she'd be willing to try them."

"Yeah?" Andre gave her a wolfish smile. "I'd enjoy seeing that." He pinched her nipple, tugged on it. "And maybe some other toys. Do you like toys, Michelle?"

The gentle probing between her legs gave Michelle the strength to open her eyes. A staggering climax and talk of nipple clamps left her mind fuzzy. "Toys?"

Nathan pushed her legs apart. "I'll bet you have a dildo." He swiped her clit with his tongue. "Maybe a butt plug too."

"I don't… Ahhhh." She spread her legs wider apart when Nathan began to feast on her pussy. "Lick me. Oh, yeah."

Andre began removing his clothes as he watched Nathan lick her pussy. "Do you have a butt plug, Michelle?"

"No. Oh, Nathan, right there. Yes!"

Now naked also, Andre crawled on the bed. "We'll have to change that. I'd love to see a plug in your ass." He aimed his stiff cock at her lips. "Your turn to suck, Michelle."

She took him in her mouth as Nathan licked her clit. Andre cradled the back of her head and slowly pumped his hips. His shaft slid an inch farther into her mouth each time he moved forward. Michelle opened her mouth wider, wanting to take as much of that delicious rod as she could.

"Damn, you do that good." Andre cupped her breast, his thumb circling the nipple. "Take it deeper, babe. Take it as deep as you can."

Michelle drew back until only the tip remained poised between her lips, then slid her mouth all the way down to the base of his shaft. She repeated the action again, and again. On the third pass, Andre gently drew his cock from her mouth.

"That feels incredible, but I'm not ready to come. Let's get Nathan up here with us, okay?"

She nodded. She wanted very much to watch Andre and Nathan together. Tunneling her fingers into Nathan's hair, she gently tugged his mouth away from her. "Come play with us."

He gave her clit one more lick and kissed the inside of each thigh. He rose and ran his hands up her thighs, her stomach, over her breasts. With each of Michelle's nipples clasped between thumbs and forefingers, he took Andre's cock into his mouth.

Michelle drew in a sharp breath. Her clit began to throb, her pussy clenched. She'd never seen anything so erotic as Nathan sucking Andre's shaft. He took Andre deep, then circled the head with his tongue. He laved the length of Andre's rod, licked his balls, then took it deep in his mouth again.

Obviously, they'd done this many times.

Sliding her hand beneath Andre's balls, she gently caressed them while Nathan's mouth moved over him. Andre looked at her. "You like watching Nathan suck me?"

"Yes."

"Does it turn you on?"

"Oh, yes."

Nathan twisted her nipples, and Michelle groaned. Moisture seeped from her channel and trickled between her buttocks. She arched her hips, trying to find some relief from the heat building between her thighs. She doubted if she'd ever been this hot. "Please," she rasped. "I need someone to fuck me."

Nathan released Andre's penis. He pushed two fingers inside her and pressed upward. Rubbing her clit with one hand, he massaged that special spot inside her. Michelle threw back her head and pumped her hips. She was so close to coming again. Just a little more…

Andre pinched both her nipples. Michelle shattered.

Moments passed while her brain cells recovered enough for her to form a coherent thought. When she managed to pry her eyes open again, she saw Nathan at the side of the bed, stripping off his clothes. Andre lay at the head of the bed, propped up by several of her throw pillows. His glorious hard cock lay against his belly, waiting for her.

He held out his hand. "Come here, Michelle."

She crawled to him and straddled his lap. Andre pulled her into his arms, kissing her deeply. He touched her back, her buttocks, her breasts, while he made love to her mouth with his tongue.

How wonderful that both her men loved to kiss.

Michelle wrapped her hand around Andre's shaft and impaled herself. Gripping his shoulders, she threw back her head and moaned. "Oh, yesssssss. That's what I need."

A slick finger slid into her ass. "Do you need to be fucked here too?"

The warmth of Nathan's breath close to her ear sent goose bumps cascading over her skin. "Mmm, I'd love it."

"So would I, but I want to watch you and Andre first."

She had no complaints about that. She began to ride Andre's cock, taking him deeper and deeper. He remained still, leaving her in total control. She moved her hips up and down, then in a circle to get the most stimulation on her clit.

Andre didn't remain still for long. Holding her hips, he thrust up into her.

"Mmm, yes," Michelle moaned. "Fuck me. Fuck me hard."

She felt Nathan spread her buttocks. She arched her back, hoping to give him a better view of Andre's shaft inside her.

"Damn, that looks good." Nathan circled her anus with his finger. "Where's your lube, baby?"

She motioned toward the nightstand to her right. "Over there. Top drawer."

Andre pulled her down to his chest and kissed her passionately. Tongues played, teeth nipped, lips worshipped as he continued to thrust into her.

A cool wetness fell on her anus. Michelle mewled as Nathan spread the lubricant over the sensitive area. He circled the small hole, dipped inside, then circled it again. His caressing grew harder, faster.

"You like this, don't you, baby?" Nathan pushed a finger inside her, then two. She lifted her hips, silently asking for more. "Oh, yeah, you really do like this. Andre's right. We're gonna have to get you a butt plug. You can wear it while we fuck that pretty pussy."

Michelle whimpered.

Nathan pushed his fingers farther inside her. "Then we'll pull out the plug and fuck your ass. You'll like that too, won't you?"

"Yesssssss."

The combination of Andre's pounding cock and Nathan's caressing fingers sent Michelle over the edge again. Her body trembled from the most powerful orgasm she'd had in a long, long time. Crying out her pleasure, she fell on top of Andre, limp as an overcooked piece of spaghetti.

A woman couldn't keep having three orgasms during sex and survive.

Andre kissed her forehead. "Can you move, Michelle?"

"Uh-uh."

His chuckle vibrated against her breasts. "How about if we help you? There's a very horny man behind you who needs some attention."

"What about you?" She kissed his neck, his shoulder. "You didn't come."

"I will, with Nathan."

Knowing she was about to see Andre and Nathan have sex gave her the strength to move. Michelle lifted herself until Andre's hard cock slipped out of her. She curled up by his side, prepared to watch whatever happened between the two men.

Nathan spread lube liberally over his rod. He hooked his arms under Andre's knees and pulled him down on the bed so Andre lay flat, his legs spread wide. Placing the head against Andre's anus, he slowly pushed forward.

"Oh God," Michelle whispered. Despite feeling thoroughly satisfied, heat built low in her tummy at the erotic sight of Nathan's cock in Andre's ass. She moved closer, peering over Andre's thigh. Nathan pushed his penis all the way inside Andre and stilled.

Michelle glanced at Andre's face. His eyes were closed, his breathing deep and heavy. She looked at his cock, still damp from her juices. He was so hard, his skin shone.

Nathan moved, pulling partway from Andre's body before pushing back inside. Andre groaned softly and arched his neck. A drop of sweat rolled down his temple into his hair. He had to love what Nathan was doing to him. She dropped kisses on his chest. "Do you like Nathan inside you?"

"Yes. *God*, yes. It feels so good."

She grasped his cock, and he groaned again. "Do you like me watching?"

Andre opened his eyes. The green irises looked like sparkling emeralds shooting heat. "Yes."

Tightening her hold on him, she pumped his rod in time to Nathan's thrusts. When Nathan picked up speed, so did she. She slid her hand up and down the hard flesh, over his balls. She paid special attention to the sensitive spot between his balls and his anus. A flick of her tongue over the head and Andre jerked. His cum flowed from the slit and ran over her hand. She didn't release him, not even when Nathan drove his shaft all the way inside Andre's ass and growled out his release.

Michelle curled back against Andre's side. He wrapped one arm around her shoulders and kissed the top of her head. In only a few short weeks, she'd found two incredible men and fallen madly in love with them. Even more incredible, they loved her too. And each other.

Michelle drew tiny circles on Andre's stomach with one fingertip. "I never suspected watching two men have sex would be so hot. Now I understand why men like watching two women together."

"Does that mean you'll have sex with a girlfriend and let Nathan and me watch?"

She frowned. "No, that's not what it means. Sheesh. Get your mind out of the gutter, Andre."

"There's nothing dirty about making love."

Nathan lay on the other side of Andre. He reached over and entwined his fingers with Michelle. "Especially when you love someone."

Andre laid his hand over theirs on top of his stomach. "And we all love each other."

"So this is really going to work? All of us together?"

"Yes, it's really going to work." Andre lifted her hand and kissed the palm. "I promise you."

A frown drew Michelle's eyebrows together. Something was different about Andre's speech. She'd noticed it earlier, but had been too caught up in orgasms to mention it. She propped up on one elbow. "Hey, what happened to your accent?"

Nathan chuckled. "Yeah, Andre, what happened to your accent?"

Andre frowned. "Shut up, Nathan."

"Time to spill it, buddy. Tell her the truth."

"It's phony?" Michelle asked. She couldn't believe he'd fooled her.

"No, it isn't phony. I really am from Italy. But my accent isn't as…heavy as I've led you to believe."

"Now I'll tell you what he isn't saying. He's lived in the States for sixteen years. His accent conveniently comes and goes. It becomes heavier when he's trying to impress a woman."

"So you used it to impress me?"

Andre grinned. "It worked."

It certainly had. She'd been charmed by his beautiful words and the lovely way he'd said them. "I'll admit I liked the accent, but you have other things that impressed me too." She slid her hand down to his soft penis and gave it a gentle squeeze.

He inhaled sharply at her touch. "You keep doing that and I'll be ready to fuck again in no time."

"So will Nathan." She'd watched Nathan's cock begin to lengthen, thicken, as she caressed Andre. "You guys really do recuperate quickly, don't you?"

"And aren't you lucky that we do?" Nathan asked.

"Very." She continued to caress Andre. "What other secrets have you kept from me?"

"Well, let's see." Nathan tapped his chin. "There's the tiny tidbit about Andre being royalty."

Michelle's hand stilled. "What?"

"I'm not royalty, Nathan. Don't mislead her."

"Okay, maybe not royalty, but the closest thing Italy has to it. His family has owned the same vineyard for nine generations. It's the largest in the country."

"You can go back nine generations?" Michelle asked, impressed.

"Roots are very important to my family. My mother has papers and documents that go back almost four hundred years."

Simply because she enjoyed it, Michelle began to caress his cock again. It quickly responded to her touch. "I'd love to look at them."

"I will take you to Italy to meet my family. My mother will love you."

"So will your brothers," Nathan said.

"That's true. I'll have to keep you far away from my randy brothers."

"None of them are married?"

"Two are. That doesn't seem to matter when they see a beautiful woman."

"I have all I can handle right here." Rising to her knees, she moved between the two men so she could caress Nathan's shaft too. It responded as quickly as Andre's. "Before we get busy again, so to speak, are there any other secrets y'all want to tell me?"

Andre shifted his hips, sliding his rod along her palm. "We have better things to do now than talk. Besides, finding out along the way will be an adventure. Don't you think?"

Michelle smiled. "Let the adventure begin."

The End

Enjoy an excerpt from:
DESTINY BY DESIGN

"Beautiful, isn't it?" Ellis sighed, running her hand along the smooth grain. "Just wait until they affix the cherry accents and apply the finish coat. It'll positively glow!"

Ellis and Remi were inspecting the wood and pre-made supports for the built-ins at the Callon & Son workshop. It's not that she didn't trust Marco, but she really needed to see and feel the material they were going to use for the piece that would become the focus of the room.

"Yes, this will do nicely," Ellis agreed, responding to Remi's wolf whistle.

"Yeah, but that's not what I'm admiring," Remi replied.

Ellis followed his gaze past the open double doors to see Marco's insolent workman striding toward them from the other side of the yard.

"Who, him?" Ellis asked.

"Yes, girl! Just look at the way his tool belt hangs all low on his hips, like he's Gary Cooper going to fight the bad dudes at high noon. You've got to admit he's hot."

"Okay, I'll give you hot, but Remi you know me. I don't go for muscle heads and this guy is practically dripping testosterone." Ellis had two good eyes. She could see and appreciate the guy's finely honed physique, but men like that weren't her type. She preferred someone like her father, a worldly intellectual who could carry on a conversation. Some of her earliest teenage crushes landed squarely on her father's young protégés and other professors from the university at which he taught music.

Ellis admired men who had a well-developed mind, who could discuss a good book, enjoy an art show and know which fork to use for salad. Men who were in touch with their emotional and sensitive sides. She suspected the he-man bearing toward them exhibited none of these qualities, as demonstrated by his language and attitude. His idea of fine dining was likely the big value meal at Burger Heaven. Ellis was sure this dude could build a nice brick wall, but could he hold a conversation over dinner? Probably not.

"Oh yeah, Simon is all Mister Man…mmm, mmmm!"

"His name is Simon? Remi, let me tell you a little secret. Despite appearances, he's a bad guy. The Simon character in books and movies always turns out to be the villain."

"For example?"

"For example, Simon Legree in *Uncle Tom's Cabin*. Hello? Evil slave master! And in the romance novel I just finished, Simon kidnapped the winsome bride of the Duke of Carberry and raped her. On her wedding night! E-V-I-L! It's a really good read, by the way. I'll lend it to you if you want. And don't forget Simon Cowell from *Idol*. He's rude and nasty."

"I counterpoint with Simon Templar, aka, 'The Saint'."

"Then there's Simon Says, who's really bossy, and Simple Simon who's just plain stupid."

"You're stretching."

"Yeah, but this Simon is a rude pig. Do you know how he spoke to me?" Ellis said in an undertone as Simon strutted to within hearing range.

"Well, I guess he can speak to you anyway he likes 'cause he's—"

"Shhhh," Ellis hissed as Simon came within earshot, sure that Remi was going to say something inappropriate about his extraordinary physique. As she watched his approach, Ellis had to admit that he had a natural air about him that shouted confidence. He really was a fine specimen, with his tousled black hair and shoulders an acre wide. His jeans, faded to a soft grayish blue, hugged his hips and muscular thighs. She wished she could get a view from the rear.

"May I help you, Miss Strathmore?" Simon asked, crossing his arms over his chest.

"We've come to see your boss. Is he around?"

"My what? My boss?"

"Yes, Marco. Is he here?"

"I'm afraid he's not," Simon smirked, looking down as if something on the ground caught his attention. He managed to compose himself before meeting her eye. "Is there something I can help you with?"

"I don't think so Mister, um… I'm sorry. I don't believe I got your name."

"Callon, ma'am. Simon Callon."

Why an electronic book?

We live in the Information Age—an exciting time in the history of human civilization, in which technology rules supreme and continues to progress in leaps and bounds every minute of every day. For a multitude of reasons, more and more avid literary fans are opting to purchase e-books instead of paper books. The question from those not yet initiated into the world of electronic reading is simply: *Why?*

1. *Price.* An electronic title at Ellora's Cave Publishing and Cerridwen Press runs anywhere from 40% to 75% less than the cover price of the exact same title in paperback format. Why? Basic mathematics and cost. It is less expensive to publish an e-book (no paper and printing, no warehousing and shipping) than it is to publish a paperback, so the savings are passed along to the consumer.

2. *Space.* Running out of room in your house for your books? That is one worry you will never have with electronic books. For a low one-time cost, you can purchase a handheld device specifically designed for e-reading. Many e-readers have large, convenient screens for viewing. Better yet, hundreds of titles can be stored within your new library—on a single microchip. There are a variety of e-readers from different manufacturers. You can also read e-books on your PC or laptop computer. (Please note that Ellora's Cave does not endorse any specific brands.

You can check our websites at www.ellorascave.com or www.cerridwenpress.com for information we make available to new consumers.)

3. *Mobility.* Because your new e-library consists of only a microchip within a small, easily transportable e-reader, your entire cache of books can be taken with you wherever you go.

4. ***Personal Viewing Preferences.*** Are the words you are currently reading too small? Too large? Too... ANNOYING? Paperback books cannot be modified according to personal preferences, but e-books can.

5. ***Instant Gratification.*** Is it the middle of the night and all the bookstores near you are closed? Are you tired of waiting days, sometimes weeks, for bookstores to ship the novels you bought? Ellora's Cave Publishing sells instantaneous downloads twenty-four hours a day, seven days a week, every day of the year. Our webstore is never closed. Our e-book delivery system is 100% automated, meaning your order is filled as soon as you pay for it.

Those are a few of the top reasons why electronic books are replacing paperbacks for many avid readers.

As always, Ellora's Cave and Cerridwen Press welcome your questions and comments. We invite you to email us at Comments@ellorascave.com or write to us directly at Ellora's Cave Publishing Inc., 1056 Home Avenue, Akron, OH 44310-3502.

erridwen, the Celtic Goddess of wisdom, was the muse who brought inspiration to story-tellers and those in the creative arts. Cerridwen Press encompasses the best and most innovative stories in all genres of today's fiction. Visit our site and discover the newest titles by talented authors who still get inspired - much like the ancient storytellers did, once upon a time.

Discover for yourself why readers can't get enough of the multiple award-winning publisher

Ellora's Cave.

Whether you prefer e-books or paperbacks,

be sure to visit EC on the web at
www.ellorascave.com

for an erotic reading experience that will leave you breathless.